D1523760

Stand Your Ground
(A Torsten Dahl Thriller)

By

David Leadbeater

Crime, thriller, mystery, action, adventure, military, war,
suspense, men's adventure, assassinations.

DEDICATION

For my wife and children,
Erica, Keira, Megan
'One day confound, the next astound.'

ONE

Of all the absurd ways to spot one of the world's most dangerous men, Nick Grant never imagined it would be over the top of a fat and juicy Five Guys burger.

Is that . . . ? Was it . . . ?

No, it couldn't be.

Could it? After so many years?

Grant hated to give up the burger, but his prey made for a far more palatable prospect.

Dulles International in Washington, DC, hummed with humanity, its gleaming floors trodden by tens of thousands, from the world-weary to the desperately excited, its open-plan shops and restaurants gleaming from wall to wall. There were Bentleys waiting to be won, tired shop assistants helpfully pointing customers to the most expensive products, coffees and pastries and specialty chocolates being served. Announcements chimed out, one merging with the next, pointing travelers to their gates. Grant found the airport hustle comforting, anonymous, and felt a moment of happiness remembering that the number of living people who knew his face and could connect it to what he did numbered less than a dozen.

Unfortunately, one of them had just crossed his path.

Grant didn't think Torsten Dahl had seen him, but he had to be sure. Dahl was an ex- Swedish Special Forces soldier – an elite warrior. To underestimate such a man would be equivalent to stabbing oneself in the back, and Grant hadn't survived twenty years of criminal activity living in a cloud of complacency. Nor had he survived two previous run-ins with Dahl by taking the veteran lightly.

Laying the burger on the tray, he slid off of his high stool and melted into the multitudes heading for Duty Free. His quarry was a tall man, broad and sporting a head of blond hair, making him relatively easy to keep track of. The real problem was maintaining his own anonymity. Grant didn't know much about Dahl's activities these days – their paths had been divided for over a decade – but he had heard that the Swede was working for the American government, part of some task force. The way the man shopped leisurely in the sundries store now, picking out tubes of toothpaste, deodorant and packets of mints, told Grant that he wasn't exactly mid-mission. It occurred to Grant then that the Swede, isolated and relaxed, might never be more vulnerable.

Except for the location, of course. It would be madness to move on a target inside a major, international airport.

As Dahl paid for his items, two children ran up to him, clutching at his coat. Girls, both of them, perhaps eight or nine years old. Their excitement was infectious, Dahl bent to hug them both as a woman approached the trio, also blond.

Grant's suspicion was confirmed: Dahl was departing on some kind of vacation with his family.

Moments ago, he'd postulated that the Swede might never be more vulnerable than while traveling for pleasure. But as he watched him now, as he saw the interaction between Dahl and the two kids and the woman, Grant realized he could be more vulnerable. He *was* more vulnerable.

Grant followed the foursome at a distance, taking infinite care to remain unseen. The Swede might be good, but Grant was no freshman. People had been trying to kill him for years, or at least lock him up, which to Grant amounted to pretty much the same thing. He still tasted gun smoke when he thought about his long-ago encounter with Dahl . . . heard the grunts and moans of his dying men . . . and then tasted bitter, personal hate when reminded of his most recent one.

As the family walked ahead of him, Grant took a quick glance at his own boarding pass, seeing that his gate also lay ahead. Wouldn't that be interesting . . . ? He entertained a vision of unknowingly sharing the same flight with Dahl, seats apart, and never, ever knowing. How many times had that happened to people? Ex-lovers? Even estranged sons and fathers. The people who sat around you on a plane always had full lives of their own, but imagine if you'd actually known them, or shared an anonymous smile across the aisle. It might stay in your memory forever.

Grant's eyebrows rose as Dahl steered his family into a gate area marked for Barbados. He didn't have to double-check his boarding pass to know they had booked the same flight.

As Grant walked past the gate area, averting his face, his mind turned to how he might profit from the situation. Profit always came before revenge, though on occasion the two could make powerful bedfellows.

Possibilities pummeled his brain like prize-fighters, each vying for his attention. In the end, only one could win, and it tied in perfectly with his current undertaking. To do it, he needed to make a call and change flights. Grant stopped at a sparsely populated gate and stood before an empty row of leather seats overlooking a stretch of asphalt and two lonesome-looking planes. He entered a speed-dial number in his phone.

"Hello?"

"Give the phone to him."

"Who is this?"

One of Vega's men, trying to be funny. "Give him the phone, or I will facilitate the removal of your funny bone and see how long you laugh."

A pause and muffled speech.

"This is Gabrio."

Gabrio Vega was the head of one of the world's largest and most violent drug cartels. Not a normal criminal – or human being – by any stretch of the imagination, Vega treated his men like family, conducted the majority of his business dealings through the Web, and employed an online security and search presence the FBI would have been proud of.

Hence Grant's open sanction to contact the man directly.

"I'm at Dulles right now and have come across something that may be of interest to both of us."

Vega took a moment to absorb that. "Does it have any bearing on our Barbados operation?"

"No, sir, I don't think it does."

"Then leave it alone. Barbados is shaky right now, and we have too much invested in there to let it all go sideways."

Grant made a quick mental calculation, then decided to press the issue. "If you'll give me one minute to explain, I think you might . . . enjoy this."

Another silence. "Enjoy?"

Grant imagined him sat behind a big Lenovo, fingers flying, the drug lord planting his specific poisons all around the Internet.

Before Grant could respond, Vega said, "You got forty seconds. And only because it's you. Go."

"Do you remember a man named Torsten Dahl?"

The words had the required effect.

"*Dime.*" *Tell me* in Spanish.

Grant had expected the change in Vega's tone. The man's last encounter with Torsten Dahl had left his brother dead and his Amazon operation in tatters. Millions, perhaps hundreds of millions, lost. Though it had been a decade ago, it no doubt felt like yesterday to the cartel chief.

"I'm looking at him right now. He's sitting with everything he holds dear in this world and about to board a plane to Barbados."

Another drawn-out silence.

"I thought you said it didn't involve our operation." Vega said quickly.

"I don't believe it does. The man's embarking on what looks to be a family vacation."

"So you what? Followed him?"

"Only inside the airport. I had no idea he was here. Pure chance we ended up on the same flight."

"Don't get on it. Follow on the next flight. My men will pick him up on arrival. I'll see you soon."

Grant couldn't help but wince. "Please make sure they're your very best. Dahl will spot an obvious tail, even on vacation, and we can't alert him to any of this."

Vega was known, somewhat affectionately by some, to hire any man willing to join his extended family, which included the unsavory and the not-so-bright. The main criterion was that they would wear a suit.

But Vega was already gone.

Grant stared hard at his phone and then out the window. What did he mean? *I will see you soon.* No way was the world's most wanted drug lord heading from Mexico to Barbados. They hadn't discussed that. Grant had never met the man in person, and quite frankly never wanted to.

He sighed. Vega had old scores to settle, exactly as he did.

This thing with Dahl suddenly began to look as if it might get very messy.

Loud.

Two outcomes Grant could little afford. He turned and

began to search for an available desk agent who could book him onto a later flight. He also began to mentally amend everything he'd imagined might work to trap Dahl. The cartel would do their own thing, regardless.

Funny thing. Here he was, not even booked on the next flight yet, but already dreaming up a plan to escape Barbados the earliest chance he got. And, in truth, already regretting his call to Vega.

Torsten Dahl found it hard to shrug off the shroud of worry that had fallen across his broad shoulders less than a half hour ago. Airports were hubs of unending motion, one face popping up in a crowd could meld with another and another, and then disappear before a man even remembered why it had suddenly, inexplicably felt important. Dahl trawled his memory, sifting through the years, through incidents that he would never speak of with his family, until a match popped up like a painted, Halloween ghoul.

Nick Grant. An English-born, well-educated man known in criminal circles as 'the Facilitator' for services rendered to an exclusive set of bad actors. Grant's title bridged a wide and pitiless gap, for he had been suspected of conspiring to commit more crimes than any book of law contained – from leaning on lawyers in pivotal trials to engineering bloody wars in the Middle East.

Dahl maneuvered around shelves and display cases as he shopped for sundries, using reflective surfaces as a backwards-facing mirror. Lightning-fast, he skimmed every face, every figure and frame. Men, women and children bobbed by, their features sparking no recognition.

Was he seeing ghosts? Had the job eclipsed all to the

point where he saw enemies lurking at every corner? Dahl had been on the job for two years straight, no breaks except for a week's leave here and there. He recalled something that had been said to him a dozen times in the last few weeks alone:

Take a break. You need it.

He'd helped avert Armageddon at least twice, not that anyone below a certain level of government would ever know, and who was really keeping count?

Continuing to shop, Dahl chose a handful of items to keep up the charade. He moved to the register, chiding himself for wasting any time that he could be spending with the three people who meant the most to him. Truth be told, it had been a long time since they'd all been together like this, and Dahl was feeling a little out of his element.

Isabella and Julia raced into the store and ran up to him with freshly washed hands, sparkling eyes and exuberant smiles. He was reminded again why he did what he did. Because every man and woman wanted just one thing out of life – to keep their family safe. But most weren't equipped with the mind-set or capabilities required to go to war and earn that safety. So Dahl did it for them. Without question. Without regret. And with no expectation of reward.

"We found a chocolate shop," eight-year-old Isabella said.

"Is it calorie-free chocolate?" Dahl asked.

Isabella turned her nose up. "What's a calorie?" She wrapped her tongue around the word with ease, another reminder of how much Dahl had missed his girls' daily development during the last few years.

"A calorie is a food unit," nine-year-old Julia explained, "that grown-ups care about a *lot*. Mom always says she counts hers."

Isabella laughed. "That's silly."

Dahl thought so too but kept his peace. He still couldn't shake the feeling of unease that had taken root in him. A quick, surreptitious glance in a nearby sunglasses-rack raised no flags.

Of course, he thought. *Because there's nothing to see . . . There's always an easier, more straightforward way to find out if you're being tracked aboard a plane.*

The nagging, persistent thoughts revolved around Dahl. As a career soldier, he trusted his instincts. Every single insightful, informative and often insensitive one of them.

His wife Johanna followed the girls into the shop, looking happy and smiley, but Dahl knew the façade was for the benefit of the children. Their long marriage was at its rockiest point ever right now . . . something Johanna and he hoped a vacation would cure. But no matter their marital woes, there was no way either daughter should be privy to it. Not at this point.

"Shall we wait at the gate?" asked Johanna.

Dahl nodded and led the way, his mind momentarily free from Nick Grant and focused on the greater task at hand: saving his marriage.

TWO

Dahl saw beauty everywhere. The bluest skies and highest palms were the softest of treats to the eye; the intermittent views of a Caribbean sea and sandy beaches were nectar, the laid-back attitude of the Bajan locals a soothing balm. Time moved differently here. Dahl could see it already. The shades of blue were deeper, richer, the yellows more golden and laced with promise. Even the music was a vibrant mix of high spirits and laughter. Isabella and Julia soon warmed to it, and seeing them happy and carefree brought Dahl a profound sense of relief.

This was already better than their flight experience in every way. He'd found himself hefting hand luggage down and smiling at the girls, reassuring them that they'd be out of the small cramped space with its below-par food and unsmiling stewardesses momentarily. Bodies had pushed against him from behind as others joined the fray. The flight attendants had finally started to smile as they saw an end to their working day.

The taxi slowed as its driver followed a wide, sweeping bend up a driveway bordered by palm trees and a high, orange-pink wall. At the very top it widened out even more as the hotel's entrance appeared – a colorfully-clad gateway to paradise. Porters hovered outside, leaning on trolleys and tourists milled all around, getting in the way. Eyes drifted over the new arrivals, but none appeared suspicious, even the ones that lingered overlong on Johanna's blonde hair. Dahl handed over a wodge of local currency to the taxi driver and then followed a porter into the high-ceilinged lobby, spotting the reception, check-out and concierge desks immediately. Isabella and Julia pointed out the way to the restaurants and shops and then they were treading between red ropes, in line to check in.

"Welcome to the Barbados Palm. How was your journey?"

Dahl presented their documents, which the receptionist ignored. "Not bad at all, thanks."

"Name?"

Dahl reeled it off and spelled it out, thinking, *You'd know that if you looked at the bloody information in front of you.*

He breathed in long and deep. *Stay calm. Relax.*

"You are with us for two weeks? Yes?"

"Yes." Through gritted teeth.

"Ah, I am so sorry. Your room is not yet ready."

Dahl tensed, feeling the stress of the flight, his marital problems, the ghost of Nick Grant and a dozen other concerns mesh together somewhere around the right temple. A heavy pulse began to throb. "Are you joking? Is that the—"

A female hand fell onto his shoulder and squeezed, and a light voice whispered into his ear. "It's okay. We can wait. We can relax. Remember?"

Dahl exhaled fast, letting it go. Of course they could wait. This was a vacation, after all.

Johanna continued her whisper. "I know you, Torsten. I see what you're doing and I respect it. I also want you to think about our family, and what this means to us. This vacation. Can you do that?"

Dahl said that he could.

"Unwind and tone down just a little. A bit more every day. I can live with that if you can."

He nodded quickly. "I'll try."

He grabbed hold of the trolley, exerting at least a little

control over his destiny, and maneuvered it into a corner beside a plush white corner seat. The receptionist told them he'd call them over when their room was ready.

Dahl grunted and checked his watch. Already mid-afternoon. He felt more than a little frazzled. Maybe it had something to do with the Nick Grant false alarm earlier. Stuck on the plane in a world of worry, he'd cited an excuse to stretch his legs and cruised the aisles, from first-class and back, searching for one face among hundreds – that one, vile face that carried bloodshed, hurt and fear to every region it visited. With every step he was ready to act, muscles coiled, mind prepped, but the connection never happened. Dahl felt immense relief at first, and then doubt followed by suspicion. Soon, he had imagined several serious scenarios, each one worse than the last, and had to physically prevent himself from making a call to the team back in DC.

Instead, he'd deposited himself back into seat 34 D and taken several deep breaths. *There is no madman on this flight. There is no . . .*

He leaned back now and managed to chill out for exactly nine seconds before Isabella landed knees-first in his lap, forcing out a groan. Julia looked on a little more seriously and met Dahl's eyes over the younger girl's head. *Kids*, she mouthed, disapprovingly.

Dahl grinned back and then grabbed Isabella and began to tickle her mercilessly until she started squealing and loudly stating that *she was eight now and not a child anymore*. Dahl apologized and stood her up with a sober face. Johanna brought mango smoothies and the four sat back to watch the comings and goings across the vast lobby until their room became ready.

Once inside, Dahl finally felt an easing of the pressure,

David Leadbeater

especially when he was able to double-lock the door behind them. It took a matter of moments to scan the apartment, check all the locks and potential weak areas, assess ingress and egress points and get a feel for the general area. Turning, he saw Johanna watching him.

"You done?" she asked pointedly.

"All present and ready to have fun," he said. "If I can remember how."

"Take your shoes off," Johanna said. "There's a start. The hotel provides free slippers."

"They do?"

Johanna handed him a set of white slip-ons wrapped in a sealed plastic bag. "Start with these. I'll show you the bathrobes later."

Dahl obliged and wandered the room, a bit more leisurely this time. The kids were checking out their own room and the twin beds. Dahl heard the balcony doors slide open and moved fast.

"Wait," he said. "Just wait."

Isabella humphed but Julia was at an age now where she understood. Dahl checked the balcony and the rails and then stood for a moment, staring down. Heart-shaped pools lay below, rippling and glistening. Adults swam lazily toward a pool bar, drinks already in hand. Palm trees shaded certain areas and flesh of every kind cooked in the heat of a slowly waning sun. Laughter and shouting and the smell of a barbecue drifted past his nostrils, and Dahl began to feel hungry.

"Can we go down?" the girls asked in tandem. "Please?"

Dahl looked to Johanna, who nodded.

He took his daughters' hands. "Let's go."

They headed out of the room and down. Dahl looped the room card around his neck. His immediate thought was to seek out food and the nearest restaurant, but Isabella and Julia wanted to head for the pool. One look

12

at their excited faces convinced him. Johanna backed it all up with a knowing smile.

"What's good for them," she said, "has to be good for us too."

"Sure. I wasn't thinking."

"Don't worry." Jo gave him a fake punch in the shoulder. "We'll keep you straight."

Isabelle and Julia ran off noisily ahead, making the hall shake in their excitement. Dahl and Johanna followed more slowly, but eagle-eyed, always watchful where their girls were concerned. As they made their way down to the pool area, Dahl again found himself thinking of that chance encounter at the airport.

Nick Grant . . . Could it have been him?

Dahl always trusted his instincts. If he were on a mission, he would have stopped everything and called in immediately with his suspicions. But today was different. The presence of family changed everything. He wanted to stay married. And not just for the kids.

THREE

Dahl leaned back and placed his slippered feet upon the short round table that stood in the middle of their balcony. Johanna sat opposite him, the two of them finally alone after making sure Isabella and Julia were tucked into bed. Johanna sipped red wine while Dahl tipped back a bottle of local brew. Darkness had fallen, but the sounds of tourists wandering and playing below had not diminished.

"Nice view," Johanna said.

Dahl looked through the balcony rails toward the beach. Beyond the sounds of revelry came the play of the surf across the sands, the soft whoosh of the waves.

"Depends."

"On what?"

"On what happens next."

"We have a problem, Torsten, and we need to talk about it."

Dahl sat forward. "There you go."

"There *I* go? What the hell does that mean? There are two of us in this relationship, in case you'd forgotten."

"All right. So why do you think we . . . have marital problems?" It was harder to say than he'd realized. It felt like admitting defeat.

"We stayed in Stockholm for you." Johanna said. "We moved to DC for you. Uprooted everything. We still hardly see you and . . ." She sighed sadly. "You're missing them grow up."

Dahl took a quick swig to hide a stab of pain. Of course she was right. One week away amounted to hours of lost moments, every single one of them precious. Children only grew up once and the changes were fleeting.

Blink . . . and you miss it.

His father told him that. Not in this context, but in a manner that spoke for all the best things in life. The good times were short and the *better* times? Well, they vanished faster. One moment you were at the center of all the good stuff – the next it was fading in your rear-view.

"What are you thinking?" Johanna asked.

"That I don't know how to make this right."

"Clearly. And we're stuck. Where do we go next?" Johanna rose and took time to pour herself another glass. Laughter and a little song floated up from below, a happy balm infusing the air.

"What do you want me to do?"

"That's not the right question. If you suffered a wound in battle what would you do about it?"

"I'd bandage it," he said. "Or cauterize it closed, depending on how severe it was."

Johanna chose to ignore the last statement. "And would it heal?"

"Yes. Eventually."

"And do you have a bandage for us?"

Dahl remained silent. The response that tempted him — *No, but I'm afraid we're at the cauterization stage* — didn't seem appropriate. It felt surreal: Here they were, on the first evening of their long-awaited vacation, discussing the collapse of their marriage. He didn't think their conversation could take a darker turn until Johanna spoke again.

"I've found myself thinking about what it would be like with somebody else." As she said it, she brushed a tear from her cheek. "I've had a wandering eye."

Dahl stood up fast and moved to the balcony, staring into the darkness of the night sky, a reflection of his heart. "Not once have I stopped loving you," he said. "Do you want me to quit my job?"

"Of course not. And I don't want to hurt you. I only say it to be honest. But something has to change."

Dahl turned to face her. "I have no idea how to . . . get us back on track, Jo. In being the best soldier I've lost something, yes, but I'm still a caring father. There seems to be some invisible barrier. How do you find the fire again, once it's lost? How do you find the will?"

Johanna wiped away more tears. "Do you know what I think the main problem is? We don't *need* each other anymore. Not like in the beginning. At first we relied on each other every day. But as time went on, we learned to function apart from each other. And once you don't need each other, you turn to other things. Maybe . . ." She shrugged. "Maybe we change it all now. Maybe we should just take a break for a while."

Dahl took his seat and reached across for her hand, suddenly convinced that he had to stand his ground. "We can work it out," he said. "Find the bandage. Make it heal. Just give it some time, some sunshine, and some sandy beach. We'll talk more . . . about us. Every night. It's good to get this out in the open, Jo. You were right to do it. Because now we know where we are."

"I'm right here, Torsten. Have been for years."

She released his hand, squeezed out from behind the small table and headed back into their room. As she curled up underneath the covers, he turned his head again toward the night sky and the shadow-strewn beach, wondering what manner of enemy might lurk out there.

He might not have the answer for his marriage tonight, but there was one thing he could do: He would keep his family safe. He would watch out for them.

All night, if need be.

The dawn be[g]
met the sky,
throwing bu[r]
with the pr[c]
Dahl an[d]
footsteps. ...
their clandestine assau...
youngsters pounced. His wife and ...
sheets with their daughters, goofing happi[ly]
eyes met.

Despite it all, and contrary to what he'd hoped, Dahl didn't feel any better about things this morning.

The breakfast buffet was lavishly spread out, the coffee invigorating. It was still early when they were all fed and watered. At the children's insistence they agreed to explore the entire hotel, grounds, shops, lobby and all. Dahl wholeheartedly endorsed their plan – the soldier in him would have insisted they do it anyway.

Always check the lay of the land, he thought. *Even the kids know it.*

As it turned out, the lay of the land to Isabella and Julia meant the placement of ice cream huts, jet skis and banana boats. Dahl let them roam while making his own recce – the questions piling up as his toes squeezed the sand.

What's hotel security like? Are they armed? How soon could the local authorities arrive in an emergency? He even looked around for the closest weapon he could improvise.

Calculations ran through his brain, glazing his eyes

w through it all. She sighed and

nd would never change; she'd known
et, as college students, for goodness'
d accepted it. Their problem was . . .
e.
ted a map of the hotel and its grounds from a
osk and ran ahead to catch up with the kids.
g was proposed, followed by a swim in the pool
some lazing on a deck chair. Dahl nodded his
reement, eyes sweeping the crowds for a certain
familiar face.

Nobody he recognized appeared among the hotel guests, causing him to wonder whether he'd been mistaken the day before.

Unlikely.

People like Dahl didn't make mistakes. Nor did enemies who survived him.

Flicking back to Nick Grant, he remembered a man who always wore expensive clothes, bespoke hats and occasionally tailored gloves. A well-bred man, articulate, who enjoyed small jokes and was intelligent and wholly mean. Something in his youth had doused any semblance of light that may have once existed within him, Dahl knew not what. Grant was a ghost, the consummate professional and a stone-cold killer rolled into one – the only twist being that he manipulated others into doing the killing and usually left the area he'd duly devastated before the real horrors began. The first time Dahl had encountered him, Grant had been facilitating a drug deal in the heart of the Amazon rainforest. All the stars were there – the head of the biggest Mexican drug cartel and half his family, the Russian ex-KGB enforcer he was dealing with, middle-men on both sides, and Grant.

Dahl and his task force had shut it all down.

Not now. Not here.

It was enough to know that he'd failed to catch the Facilitator twice, captured only a few of the cartel and killed others. It was enough to know that Grant had later been at the heart of a second atrocity, personal to the man, and no doubt many others. Dahl had other problems to contend with right now than those lying in wait between Grant and him.

The only questions in Dahl's mind now were: Had Nick Grant been on such an urgent mission that he couldn't act upon his sighting of Dahl? And had Dahl's preoccupation over his marital woes impaired his judgment?

The answer to both questions was the same. *We'll find out soon enough.*

Johanna trailed her children with a sad heart. In truth, she'd been hoping a family vacation away from the everyday rigors would help reaffirm her affections for her husband, for the bond they'd once shared. But now that they were here, the situation only confirmed her worst fear: their relationship was in serious trouble. Not only did her husband and she lack the old spark of romance; Johanna had also cared for the kids for so long on her own that she simply didn't need help. Or want it. Her husband's assistance felt more like an intrusion. A hindrance. When Torsten proposed ideas, her immediate thought was that she could do it better. She wanted to make the calls – and deserved to.

Hell, I do this every day.

In desperation, she'd told her husband that her eye had been wandering, even though it wasn't true. She'd hoped the ploy might be the one thing to pierce the shell that surrounded him. Was his job really so important? Were there not others who could do what he did? Deep inside, where a part of her heart lay unbroken, she wanted to talk it all out. *But Torsten,* she thought, *you're not* here. *Not fully with us. In your mind, you're off stalking some battlefield, buddies at your side. The kids need you and they don't see it . . . but I do.*

And soon, she knew, Isabella and Julia would too.

Despite her doubts, Torsten deserved a chance, and that was what this vacation was all about. They would continue to talk and she would do her best to understand his side. But Johanna had already determined that she would stand her ground. No compromises and no ambiguity. Not this time. Her husband would either be a family man in everything he did, or not at all. Which meant this might be their last vacation as a family.

Harsh. Possibly unreasonable. But Johanna had moved past reason. In the end, she would do what was best for her children, and this half-lived life wasn't it.

FIVE

Dahl broke the habit of a lifetime, taking a beer before lunch.

The irony of his situation did not escape him: in the field, his colleagues called him the Mad Swede. He was known as a sociable fellow with a caustic sense of humor and loyalty bordering on recklessness. To his men, he was a dependable leader who had a slightly crazy warrior mentality. When things went south, all eyes turned to him.

Here though, in the civilian world, with all the tourists and the staff and the earnest locals around him, he felt a stinging sense of inadequacy. This wasn't his milieu. Nothing here functioned as he understood it. Years of combat seemed to have eaten away a part of his humanity. Yes, he could remember enjoying Disneyland with the family only a few short years ago. Yes, there had been a time when he never wanted to leave them and return to work.

Normality.

Where had it gone? Dahl wanted it back, normality and all the fire that came with it. Every last, flickering flame. Could he kindle the blaze by force of will alone? Could he prove he was a part of this family, a worthy husband and caring father?

Johanna called to him from the center of the pool. "Get your ass in here, soldier."

Well, that was a good start.

Dahl waded among the bodies, reaching his family and ensuring they received a perfectly gentle but awesomely thorough soaking. He threw Isabella into Johanna's arms, loving the high-pitched squealing and ignoring the

21

disapproving looks of those nearby. He tried to do the same with Julia and was amazed by how heavy she was.

"What on earth have you been eating? Buffalo?"

"Whereabouts are you from in the UK?" an older guy treading water nearby asked.

It was a common reaction. Dahl had gone to an expensive college in southern England before dropping out due to the affections of a young, pretty girl back in Stockholm, much to the anger and endless chagrin of his parents. *It's the army for you, boy,* they'd threatened him.

And he'd never looked back.

"I'm not English," Dahl said with a glance at that pretty girl from years and years ago. "Actually, I don't know *where* I'm from anymore. But I do know that I'm right where I want to be."

SIX

Gabrio Vega studied the busy workplace outside his pristine clean office window, watching the men who walked and hurried and hustled there, for the most part all burly, tattooed warriors kindly asked to fit into suits that were too tight for them and to wear ties that bunched up around their thick neck muscles. Vega stared, taking in everything and nothing at all, considering what was to come and hoping his people would make it out in one piece.

They had families, these men, dependents. He would do almost anything to see them return unharmed.

That said, they stood at the commencement of one of the biggest operations of his career. It wasn't enough to remain detached inside his sparkling, state-of-the-art office, or to issue demands and kill-warrants from behind alarmed doors. Sometimes, Daddy had to come out and play.

Vega knew that his unease for the welfare of his men ran entirely contrary to the clinical detachment with which he managed his enemies. Weakness was not a trait to be displayed in any guise, but Vega considered no part of his operation a weakness. Even concern for his men. The benefit outweighed the cost. Enemies who'd underestimated him lay all around the desert; or their heads did, planted like baby cacti.

Somehow, this environment, the efficient, industrious activity before him, calmed Vega despite all its peculiarities.

Dissention was rare, and dealt with swiftly, but Vega rarely got involved in such goings-on. The rest of the world, the cartel, and his own machinations kept him focused and on the job for as many as nineteen hours a day.

Vega closed the shades of his office window and turned to the slender, perfectly quiet young man in the room.

"Dario. What do you think?"

Vega's son had recently turned seventeen. He was rangy but solid of frame, with ropey muscles and a chiseled jaw. Unfortunately, he was also a bleeding heart, not interested in learning the family trade. Vega had decided seventeen would be the boy's coming of age, the year that would make or break him. A harsh undertaking to be sure, but one already undertaken by all of Vega's extended family, who toiled and risked it for him every day.

Yes, it was time that Dario learned the ways of men.

Live or die, boy, though you do not know it yet.

"What?" the lad had other things on his mind. "I mean – sorry?"

"What were you thinking about?"

"Nothing. I was listening to the radio."

Vega kept it playing constantly and very quietly in a corner of the pristine room, but he knew full well Dario hadn't been listening to the music. Not only that, he knew exactly what the boy had been reflecting upon. His network of digital eyes saw everything.

"I may have a job for you."

Surprise registered on the boy's face like a slap. "Me? What? Why?"

"Do you not think it's time?"

Dario studied every surface in the office but did not meet his father's eyes. "A job?"

"Yes. It is what all the men do around here."

"I know that." A small jet of teen ire.

Vega didn't talk about earning respect or becoming a man. Instead, he sat before Dario, reclining in the plush blue-leather seat, and pursed his lips. "Imagine that with one job you could ascend to the place you must be. In my eyes. In the men's eyes. With just one job."

"It sounds . . . dangerous."

"Do you want to be my son?"

The question was simple, but loaded with more ammunition than a machine pistol.

"I thought I *was* your son."

Vega considered himself a calm man; he fought the urge to rage at his son. He hadn't attained the position he had today through unending compassion, but he did try to restrain the savagery at all times. He knew things that, if revealed, would shatter the boy, but all he wanted now was a reaction.

None was forthcoming.

Vega turned away from Dario, suddenly wishing for an empty computer screen and a list of names to cross off. Or maybe a triple Sony set-up and a roster of lives to destroy. Not that such wonderful creature comforts would be allowed today, not after the recent call from the Facilitator. Vega had not felt so invigorated in a long time. His brother's murder had never been properly avenged, but now Vega saw a way to honor his brother's memory the right and true way. The only way.

By destroying Torsten Dahl's family, and then the man himself.

Blood for blood, a debt dating back to a decade ago and events that remained as fresh in Vega's mind as this morning's breakfast platter.

His brother Javier had been at the heart of it all, directing operations, as always. Vega had been watching from above, so to speak, viewing proceedings as if through a lens or a computer screen. He'd often allowed Javier to take the lead on in-person operations, preferring to remain the silent — and senior — partner.

Between them, they'd run the cartel adeptly; it worked. For every enemy Javier eliminated face-to-face, Vega used his computer skills to neutralize two more.

This occasion had brought both brothers to the Amazon rainforest on a day brighter than a brazier in Hell. The humidity and constant showers had kept them drenched and both parties edgy. Vega once thought that if a monkey screeched at the wrong time during those negotiations, the entire clearing would have been obliterated in a storm of gunfire. Luckily, it never happened. Instead, it was much worse. Torsten Dahl and his clown-show fell out of the skies and stormed the clearing, ordering Vega, his brother and their men to get down on the forest floor. Vega never even knew why, or how, the Swede had found him and tracked the meeting to the clearing. The American *federales* were always on the lookout and had no doubt gotten lucky. Perhaps one of his well-treated and cherished staffers had ratted them out. In the end, it mattered little. In the end, it was far from relevant. Vega watched as Javier took one of the clowns out and scrambled away, laying down futile cover fire. To Vega's left and right, his men took Javier's foolish bravery as a signal to fight back against the impossible odds. They had caused much chaos and noise but gained little ground, doing their best to protect him, but steadily dropping around him. They had never been the brightest, the best. Put them in a room with no doors and a single locked window and they'd still take three days to find a way out. But they were still his men, dressed impeccably and family from sunrise until dawn.

Vega managed to find his brother in the dirt and vegetation as the enemy closed in, hard, grim-faced and unsmiling. One of them, the blonde he later found out was called Dahl, fought with a fury he'd rarely seen. Vega regretted not having the man on his own team even as he lined up the sights of his pistol on that blond head of hair.

Adios *to one more American Fed asshole.*

A bullet struck his gun from his hand, sending fire through his thumb joint. Vega dropped, screaming, into a pile of mulch, amazed he still lived. It was clear now that this deal and this day were falling through the cracks, headed for Hell. Vega crawled desperately, scrabbling over a still-twitching corpse, seeking the getaway vehicles they had stationed in the underbrush. Suddenly, Javier was at his side, hauling him to his feet, and they ran, brother with brother, urging each other on as they plunged through the jungle, fleeing a paramilitary force that sought to incarcerate or kill them both. Sounds of pursuit dogged them, but the Vega brothers were fast; faster than a million bullets, to Vega's then-younger mind, and invincible. Javier and he had a business to run, networks to build and electronically inhabit, viruses to plant. They would rule together forever – a deserved destiny. It came as all the more of a shock, then, when Javier screamed and fell forward, blood exploding in a cloud from his right shoulder. Vega stared first in disbelief and then in horror, finally glaring back to look at the man who dared to shoot his brother.

Not only brother. *Friend. Fellow soldier. Shield. He knew me best in all the world.*

The blond soldier, Dahl, shouted something incomprehensible. Vega wasn't listening anyway. He raised his handgun again, but Javier shot first, discharging three bullets in quick succession. They all missed the Swede, who had the audacity to remain upright and fire right back, only his three bullets making much more of an impact than Vega's brother's. The first took Javier in the chest; the second in the stomach; the third blew the top of his head off. Vega tried to cry out. Couldn't. Stunned into immobility. Every plan for the future that they'd made suddenly disintegrated. They were *gods*, were they not? More than men, surely.

As Vega watched his brother collapse, he saw the meager reality of it all, the blood and brains, the fateful moment when one man left this world and the survivor realized that the same world would carry on turning without him.

He'd looked up from his dying brother to Dahl and found himself staring down the barrel of a smoking automatic rifle.

All the time, he thought, absurdly. *I watch. Just watch. Now . . . this . . . ?*

Vega pissed himself.

Right then, right there, deep in the rainforest, the drug lord experienced loss and terror such as he had never known before. And he'd soiled himself in the process.

The Swede shook his head, stoic. Vega fell to his knees to hide the stain and threw his hands up in the air. Unmanned, petrified, he had never known such feelings existed. Only when Dahl came under attack by two of Vega's men did Gabrio see his choice: He could sit or kneel here and attend his brother's body, or he could flee. Turn coward. Run like a puppy chased by a lion.

Vega fled, and never saw any of that day's enemies, including Dahl, again. But he had to ask himself now:

Why did you never try to track Dahl down? And why are you uneasy about it now?

Vega knew why. But nobody else in the world did, or ever would. Feeling a sudden and unexpected rush of shame mixed with anger, he offered Dario a shot glass and the bottle of tequila.

"Tip one back. And remember Javier."

Dario glanced at the clock on his mobile phone. "It's early."

"*Javier.*" The single word came out in a growl, like a

sword grinding over bone, and it showed Dario exactly what was expected.

The boy drank.

Vega poured another.

"Your initiation, then. Seventeen is the perfect age, no?"

Dario's eyes widened perceptibly. "An . . . initiation?"

Vega felt the shrinking feeling inside he imagined every father must feel to see his son display reluctance to take up the family business. "A great and worthy induction. Kill the man who killed your uncle. Wipe out his entire family. Remove his bloodline from the face of the planet."

Dario stared hard, unblinking, with the empty shot glass still in hand. Vega knew he was trying to exhibit no emotion, to remain as stone-faced as the rest of his father's men, but he had no chance of achieving it.

"This is your chance, my son. Step up now. Prove you are worthy. This opportunity is fate, rising at the perfect time. Imagine the acclaim you will receive. Any boy would die for a chance like this."

Dario, whip-thin and as fetching as a young boy could be, threw out the cheap smile he'd no doubt purchased at Walmart with all the other losers. Vega didn't like it. He grabbed the boy by the neck of his jacket, bunching the material between hard fists. "You will kill this man I choose," he said. "You will succeed and save face for us all. And you will return as a valued member of *my* family. Do you understand what I am saying?"

Dario nodded.

"The free ride is over. It's time to do . . . or die."

"Um . . . when?"

"Right now."

Vega let the boy leave, returned to the office window for a moment and then buzzed in the man who now took care of the more physical side of the cartel's business. A walking insurance policy, clad in an Armani suit and trained to kill by the toughest and maddest hard-asses all around the world.

Vega exhaled with deep concern. "That boy is a mystery to me."

The man, whom everyone called Vin, remained mute, wisely choosing not to comment on his boss's son.

"I want you to go with him. As an advisor in name, of course. But supervise, alongside Grant. Grant's forte is facilitation, so let him lead and supervise until you have the Dahls. I leave it to you, but make sure both he and Dario succeed. At the worst, you must succeed alone and then report to me. And, Vin?"

"Yes?"

"Report truthfully. No sugar-coating. No half a story. I want to hear the worst of it."

"And if the boy can't come through?"

Vega shrugged. "Then he's not of my blood. You can kill him, for all I care."

Vin hesitated. "Is that your final word?"

"Sometimes the blood does not run right, Vin. It skips a generation. Javier and I, we were the same. Dario? I find myself wondering."

"And the boy's secret?"

"Tell the men to keep eyes on her. Both you and I will be in Barbados, attending to business. That doesn't mean she won't be of help to us."

"You sure you want to go?"

Vega smiled at Vin's awkward attempt to phrase the indelicate question. It didn't fit the man's personality and made Vega's loyalty for him deepen all the more. "Sometimes, my friend, the daddy is forced to keep up appearances. This is one of those times."

"It's that big?"

Vega nodded. "It is . . . nothing short of our entire future. Now, I'll be following along in an hour. Prepare everything for me."

"Done." Vin gave a half-amused smile. "It will certainly make the next few hours more interesting."

Vega followed his man from the office's cool interior into blazing sunshine, opening his face up to the skies and basking in the increasing heat, his mind awash with the images of what might and what would happen shortly.

"This is shaping up to be a most interesting day."

SEVEN

Grant's plane landed an hour or so after Dahl's, giving the Facilitator's men already placed in Barbados a brief head start for their inquiries. Barbados was a small island. If you had associations with the right men in the right places and swiped their greasy palms with a fat wad, all types of forbidden fruit could be served up on a platter. The Facilitator had done it before, many times, and would do so again until retirement or death ended his run.

A fusillade of missed calls assaulted his phone the moment the jet landed. Grant stopped outside the terminal, seated on a bench with a bottle of water, to contact his men. Dahl and family were booked into the Barbados Palm, a large, luxury resort. Grant studied the middle-distance, suppressing a shallow memory of the rainforest battle where he'd first seen the Swede – it had all been such a blur of violence and death and, even now, he wasn't entirely sure how he'd made it out. Blind luck had helped, but Gabrio Vega certainly hadn't, utterly crushed, to the point of disability, following the death of his brother.

Today, Gabrio Vega considered himself untouchable, but Grant knew otherwise. Not a single person alive was truly untouchable

It had taken little effort to locate the Swede. Now came the difficult part. Grant didn't like that this side operation of Vega's could place their main mission in jeopardy. He'd had different ideas from Vega's . . . ways to profit from the destruction of Torsten Dahl and his family. He should have known that Vega would view it simply as an opportunity for revenge.

And if the whole job went south . . . who would be to blame? Not Gabrio goddamn Vega, that was for sure.

As for the existing mission . . .

Grant sighed and upended the bottle. Their primary mission already floated on eggshells; one misstep would result in disaster for all concerned. And the list of those concerned went high up, to people who could influence world conflicts. And others who could initiate destruction with a simple phone call. One thing Grant had learned was to furnish his undertakings with a seamless escape route, and this one was no different. But even if he survived a disastrous outcome, failure damaged one's reputation. And his reputation was all he had.

More information came from his men as the rest of the day and night progressed. Then Vega got in touch via his lieutenant and his bodyguard. An even dicier element had been added to the mix – Vega was bringing Dario in.

Against Torsten Dahl? Fucking insane.

"Is this wise?" Grant pressed Vega's bodyguard in a way he would never have spoken to Vega himself. "The timescale is already amazingly tight. If one thing goes wrong, we could be looking at total disaster."

"Agreed," said Vin. "But it is our place and our jobs to make sure everything goes right. Despite Dario. You understand?"

Grant did. "I will help capture the Dahls for your boss. It would be a shame to kill them all, though. The girls – perhaps they could be merely wounded?"

"Why?"

"I could get good money for them. I'd split the take with you."

Vin grunted. "Tempting . . . We'll see how it all unfolds. Vega isn't the world's worst boss, and he's coming too."

Exactly what Grant had feared. "We can work with that, I guess."

"You'll have to."

"The man truly has no idea how difficult it is to organize something like this."

"Email the complaints department."

"If only, eh?" Grant tossed away another empty water bottle. *God, this place was hot.* "So just to confirm . . . the men are organized and about to cause a terrorist incident. Would you like one more crack at your boss, try to turn this around? I could just as easily engineer a quiet extraction."

"Vega wants it in their faces, big, messy and loud. It will help with the . . . other matter."

Grant didn't push. The die was already cast. To question any aspect of Vega's plan now would lead to a cold, ragged hole in the ground. It always fascinated Grant how a powerful man could suggest a job, happily accept the finalized structure and then change the parameters at will, all the while expecting everything to coast along smoothly. The same thing happened the world over, and in every type of job imaginable.

The boss is a dick, Grant thought. *No matter where you work.*

"Right. Well, we're ready to go here."

"Then go. We're already on our way."

Grant ended the call and remained still for a while longer. Parameters changing was one thing, but this was outright madness. The way Vega insisted on proceeding was dangerous. Volcano-diving dangerous. Everyone involved was likely to get burned.

Grant called the leader of his local men. "Go get them and make it loud. Motörhead loud."

The merc looked blank. "What's that? Something about a motorhead?"

Grant shook his head at the intrusion of youth versus age. "Never mind. Just don't forget this is about Dahl and his family. No one else."

"What if people get in the way?" a hard-edged voice asked.

"If they get in the way, blow their bloody heads off. This is war. I've paid off enough of the local rozzers to fill a tour bus, so you'll have help."

"Detectives too?" the mercenary asked.

"Every level. Every category. Now go get 'em, my son."

"Out."

Grant clicked off with a sigh, thinking about the next step, and the ones after that.

Tomorrow was going to be a long and challenging day.

EIGHT

Torsten Dahl soaked it all up – the sun's high, revitalizing diffusion, the easy chatter and laughter, the neighboring kids whooping it up in the pool. Johanna remained aloof, but not in a mean way. Dahl could tell she was hopeful, anticipative even, but she wasn't about to make the next move. The ball was entirely on his side of the net, clasped in hand, ready to be served. An opening ace would be good.

He shifted, slightly uncomfortable in nothing but swim shorts. Real life usually found him wearing an entire plethora of outerware: under-vests, jackets and bullet-proof vests, ammo belts and utility straps, thick trousers and boots, helmets and night-vision goggles. In the pool, he felt more than a little underdressed. And his war-wound scars attracted attention, not all of it good.

Johanna asked if he wanted a drink and then swam to the poolside bar to order two South Seas cocktails. Made up of crushed ice and a splash of flavoring, they contained very little alcohol, which suited Dahl fine. His wife made her way back and he watched her closely, enjoying the sight of her body clad in a turquoise two-piece, and then feeling angry when she smiled at a hovering waiter, the man-boy's eyes roving a bit too greedily over the light-skinned blonde.

Johanna handed him a drink. "Jealous?" Her smile beamed like a second sun.

"Insanely." He sipped, wishing he could kiss her on the lips. Attraction had never been a problem for them. Relating to one another was a different thing.

"See the kids?"

Dahl nodded. Isabella swam slowly, practicing her frog-kicks, while Julia dipped her head below the water and tried to keep her eyes open. Everyday moments like this were rare for Dahl and he knew he wanted more of them.

He stepped out of the pool with Johanna, moving to their shaded sun-loungers to finish their drinks.

"Would you like to talk more now?"

"Is there anything more to talk about?" Johanna studied the far reaches of the grounds, toward the trees that lined the beach. There, tourists lounged and played and read Kindles under parasols that glowed in a riot of color.

"Surely we have enough here to try and make it work. Do you really want to start all over again?"

For the first time Dahl saw a tiredness steal into his wife's eyes. "God, no."

It was a puny foundation to build on, but it was more substance than he had a minute ago.

Isabella came up then and demanded that Mommy – an Americanism she'd picked up during her time in DC – join her back in the pool. Johanna glanced at Dahl for his acceptance; he nodded, pointed at his cocktail, and said he'd be along in a minute. What he actually needed was a coffee with cream, and he'd just spied a nice place where he might be able to find one. Standing up, he eased out a few kinks and then set off. A rooftop café sat atop one of the hotel's lower roofs and looked like a good vantage point. Dahl waved at his family and then set out, flip-flops slapping against the concrete. He moved aside for a fast-moving waiter holding a silver tray bristling with multi-colored drinks above his head on an upturned palm, watched a holiday rep breeze by and held a door for an older woman toting a thick cane. Inside, the hotel was hushed, its surfaces shiny or see-through, its corridors traipsed by tourists ranging from the downright bored to the ecstatically eager.

He took the elevator up to the rooftop and emerged into the light.

The café was small, a timber-roofed hut constructed over a round bar, but its extremities offered fine views around the entire resort. Dahl noticed that they offered light bites, and thought it would be a good place to bring the kids. He got a coffee at the bar and headed over to the nearest rail. The pool lay below, Jo and the kids splashing each other, and beyond them and the pool a patch of verdant grass, a row of palm trees and a wide sandy beach. Tranquil blue waters rolled further out, the waves seeming to crest in slow-motion. Dahl prowled the café's perimeter, examining the property's left and right boundaries, which were protected by high wire and overgrown trees through which the next hotel could be seen. To the east, the balcony looked across the entrance, the wide, sweeping driveway and outer lobby always a bustle of activity. Dahl found a seat and took the weight off, settling back until the plastic chair complained. He smelled the good, strong coffee and took a sip, relishing the flavor. His eyelids slipped closed beneath the dark sunglasses as a sense of relaxation tiptoed all around him. When he opened his eyes, he was still looking at the hotel entrance, but something had changed. Four police cars had turned up.

Dahl put the cup down and leaned forward. *Four?* That was a significant number. A sense of fatherly fear twisted down and around his spine. He rose to his feet without taking his eyes off of the emerging policeman. One of them looked to the rooftop café, catching the eyes of the people who watched from up there, and then looked away. The cop's face seemed strangely expressionless. Grim, even. Dahl quickly scanned the rest of the hotel compound and found nothing obviously amiss. Reception lay beneath a concrete dome below him, but an outer door led to the pool and beach areas. He studied that now, moving casually to the steps that led down. A youth walked out, bright red headphones on, seemingly unconcerned. A mother struggled out with an oversized stroller, then walked away, harassed but happy enough.

Perhaps . . .

Perhaps what? The cops' arrival could be anything from a security check to a nasty domestic to a chance drowning. It could be—

The rear lobby door opened again. This time Dahl saw a long line of tough-looking, stern-faced men walk out, their waist-length coats and jeans harshly out of place here, each individual's body language speaking of purpose rather than repose. Three other men near the lobby door turned dubious looks upon each other.

Dahl saw the tell-tale bulges under the coats, the glint of metal impossible to hide under the midday sun. Were the cops looking for them, or were they cops themselves? Dahl didn't wait to find out. He ran down the short flight of steps, three at a time, kicking the flip-flops off and hitting the ground barefoot. Running hard, he skirted the sun-loungers and parasols, shouting at people to get the hell out of there. The risk was too great not to warn everyone he could.

Poolside was a mess: men, women, boys and girls wading through the shallows as they tried to decide what all the commotion was about. Dahl didn't stand on ceremony, plunging through them and shouting at the top of his voice, warning of men with guns. He'd seen at least eight.

He looked for his family and failed to find them.

"Jo!" he cried. "Iz! Where—"

The crowd parted in front of Dahl, and his family appeared dead ahead, regarding him with frightened eyes and probably wondering if he'd finally gone mad.

"Men with guns!" he shouted. "Here. Now."

39

The chaos around him multiplied as the crowd took heed of his warning. Legs and arms pumped and water sprayed in all directions. Dahl scooped up Isabella and Julia and yelled for Johanna to follow. He waded hard through the deeper water and then faster into the opposite shallows, leaping off the small ledge that bounded the pool onto wet concrete. Screams battered the air, a shrill expression of absolute fear. Keeping himself between the men and his children, Dahl chanced a fast glance back.

Mayhem. Figures raced and collided and fell and leapt to every side of the pool, dripping water and seeking safety. Many followed Dahl, seeking the shelter of the extensive grounds, beach and sea that lay ahead.

For long, fearful, endless moments, high notes of terror competed with the pounding of dashing feet and barging bodies.

Then it all changed. Deep, heavy gunfire rang out, and the real terror began.

NINE

It was one thing to run for your life when you thought someone might be about to commit a reprehensible act; it was quite another to flee the sounds of approaching gunfire. Dahl's first act was to bring Johanna ahead of him and scoop up his daughters in his arms so they could move faster. What more could he do? Here they were in bikinis and swim-shorts, no communication devices and no money. No identification. Naggings of utter fear picked at his brain – those memories of Grant – but he quashed them, instead pounding along a gently curving walkway amid waist-height hedges, keeping low and moving as quickly he could while carrying the children. As they ran around the pool area, a man barged into his left-hand side and bounced off, falling to his knees. A woman sprinted past to the other side, almost lost her footing but then leapt clear an instant before she would have gone sprawling. Behind, chaos clattered with panicked cries and the chatter of more gunfire.

"We'll be okay," he whispered to the girls. "Don't worry."

Beyond the pool, he could feel the children trembling against his arms. This, more than anything, sent bolts of guilt and agony running from his brain to his heart. His girls were eight and nine. They should remain innocent of what could and might happen, of debilitating, terrorizing fear, for at least a few more years. He clung to them tightly though his arm muscles already burned. But his arms would have to fall off before he let go of his children.

A smattering of chaise lounges and accompanying parasols around the pool afforded the running crowd a false barrier. Bullets sped among them, blasting chips from wooden slats and destroying umbrella stands. Dahl swerved aside, now taking a longer route as he anticipated that the gunmen were closing. A plan formed. Open, half-drunk bottles shattered atop tables as bullets struck them. Rucksacks fell to the floor, adding to the obstacles. Towels flapped incongruously under fire. So far, nobody had veered with Dahl, and he found himself running alongside Jo in a strange solitary world for a few moments, hidden by greenery but protected by nothing. The hotel's walls loomed over the top of the hedge, bright under the midday sun, but even those were pockmarked, marred by the attackers' bullets. Out into the open again, and the beach vista now spread out before him, a serene invitation contradicting what came from behind.

"What do we do?" Johanna's words reached his ears, her voice ragged but desperately trying to stay calm for the kids.

"That way. Just a little farther and we'll have some space."

Dahl steered them in the direction of a broad freestanding cocktail bar, remembering how extensive the hotel grounds were. The bar's brick-tiered walls would help shield their getaway. The two adults ducked within as more gunfire rang out. Other people ran among them. A wall of branded bottles and polished glasses began to pound in time to a hail of bullets. Glass exploded into the air, showering the area with fragments. Luckily, Dahl and Johanna were beyond its range and kept sprinting, though the fury of the assault slowed Johanna, and thus Dahl too.

"Keep going," he gritted. "Don't stop for anything."

Out of the corner of his eye, he suddenly glimpsed dark, running figures passing the pool. A pair of gunmen flanking the scattering crowd. A split-second glance showed them firing their weapons into the air as their eyes tracked his family.

An elemental dread inhabited Torsten Dahl – his worst fears made real: These men were here for him. Ordinarily, on any normal day, he would have figured out a way to end it, to take them out of the game, something he'd done a thousand times as a soldier. Today, his world was a wholly different place. Even if he could stash the kids somewhere, their pursuers might still find them and use them as leverage.

So Dahl wouldn't take a chance, not today. Maneuvers spun through his mind, but he could act on none of them. Ways out presented themselves, but they all came from the perspective of a soldier, not a parent. The hot concrete passed beneath his bare feet and the sun burned down; waves washed across the far beach.

And Dahl spun in purgatory.

What to do?

In the end, he was left with no option. The two closest armed men swerved in his direction, aiming to intersect Johanna's run. Dahl gauged the distance of those behind the closing pair – the only reason he could imagine for their delay was that they were enjoying scaring the vacationers – and called out for Johanna to stop. She pulled up quickly as Dahl slammed on the brakes and deposited the kids at her feet in the span of three heartbeats. Then he whirled, rising to meet the oncoming challenge. Already, he believed intuitively that they were here to capture, not kill. His pursuers' eyes and body language betrayed it. Nick Grant had sent these men. He had a vast score to settle that he intended to do at his leisure.

The worst kind of debt to repay.

The men approached within ten, then five feet. *Perfect.* Hand to hand was more to Dahl's skillset. A moustached man wearing wraparound sunglasses pointed his gun barrel at Dahl, but he was having none of it. Sweeping the weapon aside with one hand, he let fly a fist with the other. The moustache whipped to the side as the neck turned and a cheekbone shattered. A healthy yell confirmed the man's utter surprise. The second man slipped around the first as he fell, swinging a rifle-butt at Dahl that caught him a glancing blow across the forehead. Blood flowed and Dahl blinked, head suddenly pounding.

"Bad move."

"Don't think so, man. Where's *your* back up, eh? Still in DC?"

This told Dahl quite a lot.

Still concentrating on three separate sectors – the kids, the rear assault and the ongoing skirmish – he placed both hands over the man's wrists and wrestled with the butt of the rifle. His opponent was strong, forearms bulging with muscle, but Dahl was stronger, grunting as he twisted the man against his will. The butt came around. Dahl pulled and then pushed suddenly, surprising the man. The force of the thrust loosened his grip and sent the weapon hard against his teeth and lips. He sputtered and the rifle spun away, useless. Dahl delivered another haymaker, stunning him. By this time — Dahl estimated that less than a minute had passed — the first man had partially recovered. As he rose again, Dahl scooped him up, throwing him over a shoulder. Parasols and deck chairs shattered as the attacker landed among them, head first. His deep, ragged groan told Dahl he wouldn't be getting up any time soon. Johanna dragged the wide-eyed kids away, instinctively moving toward the beach and shielding them from the worst of the battle. Dahl spun to check on his second attacker, blood now smearing the man's mouth and chin. He had only moments.

"What do you people want here? With all these people?"

A grimace was his only reply at first. "Who says we want them?"

Not the right time for this, but an affirmation, at least.

Dahl gauged that his time was well and truly up. He jabbed a foot in the man's face. When he stumbled backward, Dahl followed with a kick to the chest and stomp to the head, ensuring this enemy would not return to the chase soon. As he turned back to his family, another military mantra speared his brain.

Get their weapons. But family needs cut through first.

"Torsten!" Johanna screamed. "Let's go!"

Both Isabella and Julia cried out too, in reaction to their mother's fear. Dahl moved to them quickly and gathered his family in a huddle. "Be strong," he said, mostly for Johanna's benefit. "Be tough like soldiers and we'll get out of this."

"We're not fu—" Johanna started to say, then caught herself, tears leaking from the corners of her eyes.

"C'mon," he said calmly and picked the kids up again. "Let's run."

They set off like Olympic sprinters out of the blocks as booming salvos shattered the afternoon at their backs.

TEN

As Dahl took off again, a disturbing new thought started to twine, serpent-like, through his mind: *Could Johanna step up to protect their children?* He would have to fight, and he'd have to do it in front of his daughters. Dahl was coming to terms with that now. But could his wife plumb the depths of her capabilities and step up beyond anything she'd ever imagined? If not . . . they were in even poorer shape than he'd feared.

As Dahl and his family swept through a set of cabanas and more loungers, he became aware of a snuffling against this chest, and looked down to see Isabella staring up at him.

"Don't worry," the words almost choked in his throat. "We'll be okay."

A new building appeared ahead, in the center of a winding path. Called The Rum Shop, it offered only false shelter, but Dahl decided to use it to throw any spotters off. The place would have a back entrance and they could use that. The door was already open. He steered Johanna inside and then crashed through, kicking it shut behind him. Abruptly, the sounds of gunfire lessened and the human spirit tried to assure the uninitiated that they had discovered a sanctuary

"There." Johanna pointed to the high, oak counter. "If we're quiet they'll pass by."

Dahl shook his head. "We keep moving. Situations like this – you stop, you die.

"Don't say—" She stopped herself.

Dahl ignored Johanna's tearful glare, hugged the children even closer, and pointed to the back of the store. "Through there. Find a door."

He paused for a second to peek through the door behind him. Back towards the hotel, the scene was a snapshot from Hell. The high façade towered over all, dozens of its guest-room windows shot through, glass cascading down as he watched. Palm trees swayed across the entire panorama of twisted, broken chairs and tables piled in haphazard array, umbrellas and chaise lounges thrown askew, men and women in swim-clothes crawling among the debris or trying to hide amid the pools, bottles and glasses and personal belongings scattered and half-destroyed, incongruous items like sunscreen and baseball caps lying forgotten.

Dahl turned and followed Johanna, who had found the rear door.

"Exit low," he whispered. "Stay calm."

She did, leading him down a path through a thick hedge that bordered another meandering path. Certain they hadn't been seen, Dahl told Johanna to keep going, but at a slightly slower pace.

His arms were burning from the strain of his daughters' weight, but he told himself to focus on what they needed: an alternative way out, or a reliable refuge.

The beach emerged at the end of the hedged path ahead, white sands stretching wide in both directions, large areas still showing signs of that morning's early rakings. Dahl saw a crowd running to the right and stragglers to the left, and knew his earlier nucleus of a plan would now grow to fruition.

Isabella's voice broke his focus. "Are we safe, Dad?"

Julia answered quickly. "Don't be silly. Just shut up."

Dahl knew what effect that reply would have. Of course, he couldn't scold Julia, not when they were running for their lives, so he held his girls more closely. "To the right, Jo. Keep your head down."

Following a trail of footprints, they sprinted across the

sand. Its heat transferred instantly to Dahl's exposed soles, but again he fought through the pain. The kids grew even heavier as the sand grew deeper, each step grueling punishment. Dahl looked back once they'd cleared the hedge line.

The sight tore a chunk from his soul.

Ten men burst from two tree-lined pathways, most of them clad in chunky, black jackets and camo trousers. They held their guns easily, betraying an alarming confidence that spoke of careful planning and expectancy of escape. Dahl liked the situation less and less with each passing second.

Something else then accelerated his downward spiral: a face he recognized and almost expected – the face he'd dreaded – stepped out into the open. Nick Grant. Dahl almost missed a step, caught himself just before sprawling headlong. Grant scanned the beach for just a moment before settling unpitying eyes on the running family.

No mercy. No holding back. Dahl knew that now. Even if he hadn't met Grant before, he knew the man's reputation. Even if he hadn't known that, he saw it in the set of his body, the frank, coldblooded stare.

Dahl clung to the two things that meant the most to his life and picked up speed.

"Don't stop, Jo. Just keep moving."

"My feet hurt."

"Then pick them up. And *run!*"

His deliberate drama galvanized her to a quicker pace as shouts pierced the clamor behind them. Dahl chased the footprints of previous runaways, bending his route slightly seaward as he saw something on the horizon.

Ahead, two figures jogged toward them. Dahl felt his adrenalin fire for just a moment before realizing that these two were in fact policemen. Still, an inner voice told him to trust no one. The gap between them closed fast;

neither cop reaching for his belt nor moving his hands out of sight. Dahl shouted as soon as the men approached within earshot.

"Terrorists! Shooting at the hotel and guests! They're right behind us!"

He pitched his voice to what he hoped was the correct level of terror, enough to spur the cops into action. "Call it in," he called as they looked past him. "I counted at least ten men."

Disbelief lit one cop's face, unease the other's.

Hadn't they questioned the other escapees and received the same information? The pair couldn't tackle ten men alone; they should already have been on the blower.

"Look—"

They did, and as they stared past him, incredulity lit their features. Dahl saw inexperience and real fear and knew they were in serious trouble.

"Come with us," he said, still moving ahead. "You can call it in as we run."

He knew time was fleeing faster than the final death of day.

They didn't move, so Dahl kept running past them; he couldn't waste more time cajoling these men at risk to his family. A volley of shots rang out from behind. Dahl glanced back as both cops cried out, twisted and fell, their shirts shredded and bleeding. The assault team was down on one knee, the Facilitator among them, taking aim at the two cops. Again, Dahl's immediate thought was to wonder why he still lived, why the killers hadn't trained their weapons on his family. Clearly, he'd been correct: Grant wanted them all alive. The reasoning behind that couldn't be good.

Johanna's scream spurred him on, made his feet pound into the sand. If Grant were here to avenge his old supposed debt – Dahl couldn't think of any other reason

– then they'd never be safe until the Facilitator himself were dead. But that scenario didn't sit right with Dahl. Grant only showed his face and traveled to a particular country when the deal at hand was vastly important. Profitable. Could the Facilitator be juggling two missions? It had to be. Even if Grant had tracked Dahl here from the start, Dahl couldn't imagine him marshalling such resources for the hunt. Not alone. Not unless he expected payment in return.

The real Dahl rose up in him then, the Mad Swede, perfectly controlled rage pounding at his gut, inciting him to action. But the Mad Swede would already have weapons in hand. The Mad Swede wouldn't have been caught out on the open beach with his family. In truth, the gunmen were too far away anyway, and his family too exposed.

He ran on, encouraging Johanna along, sensing rather than seeing the pursuers picking up their own pace now, closing the gap. In his peripheral vision, he saw the two downed cops still crawling, still alive with survival instincts kicking in. A minute later and four more shots rang out.

The cops had been executed in cold blood, right there on the hotel beach. An unnecessary execution by men who – more than uncompromising – were cruel.

Ahead, the jumble he'd seen earlier on the horizon grew clearer, confirming his hopes.

Boats.

With an escape plan now firmly in mind, he ran harder, ignoring the spasms in his strained arm muscles, urging Johanna to greater speed with every charging step.

ELEVEN

Dahl practically threw Isabella and Julia feet-first into the last speedboat on the strand, the one closest to the ocean. He yelled at Johanna to jump in, already spying the keys dangling from the ignition, and understanding why. Hearing gunfire, a panicking man might abandon the boat and run away on foot, seeking town and the safety of buildings and police stations rather than heading straight out to sea, where safety was just as fragile.

No gunshots split the day apart, but Dahl didn't have to look back to know Grant and his men remained hard after him. If they wounded Dahl, it was all over, but even that option appeared to have been ruled out by Grant . . . or whoever was calling the shots. Still . . . best not to test them.

He pushed the rear of the craft hard across the sand, telling Jo to get ready at the ignition. Isabella and Julia hunkered down, fitting their bodies almost beneath the seats, their tiny forms so fragile that Dahl experienced a rash surge of helplessness. He turned his panic for them into fury, driving his shoulder into the boat's stern, shoving it across the wet sand and into the foaming breakers. Water splashed him. Wet sand squeezed between his toes. An incoming wave almost toppled him, but Dahl held on.

"Nowhere to run, Dahl!" A voice rang out. "Might as well stop there."

Dahl ignored it, still pushing.

"We'll get you sooner or later. The city is ours."

Dahl ignored Grant's call, concentrating on his family. Johanna perched over the wheel as if searching for a portal to another world. At a word from Dahl, she turned the key, bringing the small engine to life.

"Now get us going."

Johanna's shoulders slumped, the sobs echoing like admissions of defeat.

Dahl raised his voice. "Jo! Get us going!"

"I can't," she whispered, shuddering. "I just can't."

He cursed silently, understanding that his wife was suffering the mid stages of shock, the trauma of panic and fear immobilizing her. He pulled himself over the stern, leaped over the seats and nudged her gently aside. One twist and the engine roared to life. A tweak of the throttle and the craft surged ahead, surfing the rolling waves. For the first time, Dahl had at least a partial way out. The next decision would be pivotal.

"Can you pilot the boat?" Dahl asked Jo.

One look at her red, tear-streaked face told him the truth much more clearly than the mumble that escaped her lips. Here they were, alone in their swimsuits, pursued by assassins on an unfamiliar island, not knowing whom they could trust. The outlook was bleak. Understandable that his civilian wife could not function.

He kept the boat close to shore, taking a quick glance back to shore at the crew chasing them. Grant was clearly visible, the leader of the pack. Dressed impeccably as always, he stood out now, uncharacteristically, as the odd man. The rest wore camo pants and t-shirts covered by black military-style jackets. Dahl had seen them a thousand times, but didn't think these were lined with the bulletproof plates that were available. Some mercs would rather be comfortable than remain breathing, it seemed, but that was nothing new. Dahl's eyes roved over the weapons: an assortment of AK's, HK's and even less accurate hardware. Everything he saw told him that Grant – the best of the best – had been forced to assemble a team from whatever was available. He'd been hasty. He'd had to make do. An improvisational hunt, started at Dulles, no doubt. That worked in Dahl's favor. And made him suspect that Grant wasn't alone in this after all. Added to the many questions now haunting him was, *Who* had helped Grant amass this team. The men's professionalism did not, frankly, rise to Grant's usual standards. If Grant had organized this hunt alone, he would have come prepared, backed to the max by men who knew their job.

Grant and another, equally or more powerful individual. Both after Dahl and his family. Their hunt spurred quickly by a chance sighting at Dulles. Still . . . to have this many men at the ready, on Barbados, of all places? The puzzle would make little sense, Dahl knew, until he had all the pieces.

Dahl looked ahead, telling Johanna and the children to stay low. The beach narrowed past another property and then swept further inland. His mental map of the island was incomplete but did contain parts of the local landscape. The ocean around them was by no means empty; small sailboats with masts drifted to and fro with no signs of life aboard. Red- and blue-topped umbrellas lined the beach to the right and Dahl saw an exit off the beach, a makeshift path that led into a busy area of town, somewhere near the Harbour Lights Night Club. This was Bayshore or Pebbles Beach, then, a tourist hotspot and a great place to get well and truly lost.

Dahl considered the choices. Yes, they could power out to sea, become a speck on the horizon, but Grant would already be anticipating that. Heading further out would only make them more vulnerable if Grant commanded any significant resources whatsoever.

Dahl opened the throttle and aimed the nose of the craft at the beach. They stood a far better chance ashore, and Grant's men now lay far behind.

"Get ready," he said. "We're heading inland."

Johanna turned those red eyes upon him. "Can't we talk to someone? Where are the authorities, for God's sake?"

Dahl understood that complaining helped decent people make more sense of their situation. "We'll find somebody who can help. But first we have to reach town."

The speedboat sped among the shallows now, then struck the beach hard, bouncing slightly as it skimmed the sand. Isabella and Julia jerked forward but Dahl was already there, protecting their heads. As the boat shuddered to a stop, he pulled them out. "This time," he said, "you run *with* me."

Johanna climbed out, lost her footing and then rose again. The fight was not inside her, not today. She was so far out of her element that she might have lost all sense of self; she was running past empty.

"That way."

He moved between the umbrellas, slogging up the sandy beach. Sunshine beat down upon his shoulders. Emptiness surrounded them for the most part, but there were a few other stragglers and shapes moving within a stand of palm trees and greenery to the right. Dahl couldn't physically help the bystanders, and some soldiers — many of them – would remain mute to conceal their own location, but Dahl couldn't bring himself to do it. He shouted that they should get the hell away from the area. Return to their hotels, even.

No answers were forthcoming. The danger hadn't reached them, yet.

As the sand evened out and they approached the path, Dahl's thoughts turned to the authorities Johanna had mentioned. Grant might well have paid a certain number of them off. He had the money—that was sure. The question was whether he'd had sufficient time – or whether Grant or a partner already had a foothold in Barbados. Dahl couldn't think of a reason why they would, but, regardless, he couldn't fully trust anyone – even an innocent cop might lead them inadvertently to a conspirator.

They ran down a tree-lined avenue, coming out alongside a brick wall topped by black railings. The small car park was full, but not with vehicles. People stood outside, some apparently oblivious of what had transpired not too far away, others clearly aware and looking around nervously. The approach of sirens had triggered their awareness. Perhaps gunfire as well. The worried crowd's presence only added to Dahl's uncertainty.

"There," Johanna panted. "A cop."

Dahl grimaced, realizing that it was dangerous for them to be traveling as a family. They'd stand out like thorns on a rosebush. But separating would be madness. Try as he might, he couldn't think of a single fact that lay in their favor.

"Cops could be paid off," he said. "We need to lie low and find a way out."

Johanna regarded him in shock. "What do you mean – *paid off?* Are you—"

Dahl cut in. "In real life, people can be corrupted. Police forces are no different."

Her face still registered disbelief, but they didn't have the time. Dahl would have loved to explain it all, lay out every possibility and potential misstep, but Grant was coming and the only cop he could see had just set eyes on them.

Shit.

Dahl ushered his family along before the police officer picked them out amid the crowd. The gathering now consisted of many who had escaped the hotel and somehow saw this solid vestige of normality as a refuge. True, more cops were arriving, but Dahl saw little reason to linger here. It was now well past midday, approaching mid-afternoon; Harbour Lights was a nightclub and unlikely to be open yet. Dahl kept Isabella and Julia close and pulled Johanna along behind. His wife was silent, unhelpful, but Dahl put any anger he might feel aside – she wasn't trained as he was, couldn't react like he could, and he understood that.

Nearing the club, he saw that he'd been wrong. Its doors were ajar, people slipping in and out. Maybe they'd opened in response to police pressure . . . or actually never shut. Dahl didn't know, but at that moment he saw a figure that ignited a spark of hope.

She could help.

Still conscious of all the roving eyes, Dahl pushed a little harder, parting the throng and making a bee-line for the figure. Their eyes met and the woman smiled. She was a brunette with every single strand of hair scraped back into a huge bob that gave her the appearance of having a garden ornament affixed to her head. With her well-pressed, red jacket, gold badge and thick clipboard, she certainly looked the part.

"Can I help you, sir?"

Dahl approached the holiday rep with immense misgivings, but at the same time understood they weren't in a position to keep on running. It was time to bury the soldier's instinct, think of his family and ask for help. "I believe we're being targeted," he said. "By the gunmen at the Barbados Palm. You've heard, yes?"

The woman's expression indicated that she had.

Dahl indicated his wife and daughters. "Can you help?"

He hadn't chosen the woman at random. A good holiday rep would have intimate knowledge of the island, good contacts with police and authorities, and most importantly, a first-rate rapport with the locals. Dahl needed his family to disappear until he could call DC for backup. Of course, the call wouldn't take long, but the backup would.

The holiday rep took an unconscious step back. "You think they're targeting *you*? Please don't worry, sir. The authorities have this in hand. The police are here and—"

"You don't understand." Dahl dipped his head, drawing her face down with him. Unconsciously he reached for his own ID before remembering he'd left it back at the hotel. "Look, I realize this sounds insane but you have to help me. My family," he indicated the children and Johanna, "are being hunted."

The woman's face withdrew once more, glancing to either side. Dahl knew exactly what she was thinking. He'd seen it a thousand times. The distraught tourist. The panic-stricken dad. Suddenly, everything was about them and the safety of their kids; they only imagined the worst happening and all they wanted was to get away from this place, to get home and hold their family close.

"Wait," he said softly. "I don't have my ID, obviously, but I'm a special agent from Washington, DC." He was finessing the truth a little but staying within the boundaries of fact. "We're here on vacation, but these men . . . these gunmen, they've come after me personally."

The woman stood stock-still, but her eyes locked with his. Dahl had been trained to decipher body language, and he could tell that she wanted to believe. He hugged Isabella and Julia to his side to speed things up. The tears on their cheeks brought compassion to the woman's face.

"Follow me."

Dahl did as she asked, unused to following. The holiday rep led them into the club's dim interior, awash with shadows and nicely air-conditioned, and then stopped near the center of the large room. Dahl saw only a few people milling around, a barman polishing glasses and one or two drunks nursing their amber nectar.

"You shied away from that policeman," the woman said quite bluntly. "Why?"

Dahl knew the only reason she'd entertained his story was because of the otherwise inexplicable presence of his family. "The person we're dealing with . . . he has money and connections, even with the authorities. I can't risk . . ." He fell silent, emotion choking off the next few words.

"You're saying the police are looking for you too?" Now the rep looked a little scared, positioning her clipboard across her chest.

"Not all," Dahl said simply. "Only the ones who take bribes."

Johanna spoke up for the first time. "Can we go to a booth or something? This is crazy, standing out in the open."

Dahl tended to agree, but also knew the holiday rep wasn't about to join them in a shadowy corner. "Believe us or not," he said bluntly, "but we need your help, and we have to move. The gunmen won't be far behind."

"What do you want me to do?"

"Nothing that will put you in any danger. But we need a phone, and a place to hide."

"A phone is no problem. I can—"

And then her eyes widened and Dahl saw the approach of utter devastation.

TWELVE

Dahl spun on a dime. The man entering the club's front doors was the cop Dahl seen earlier, his gun now raised.

"Wait—"

The shots rang out clear and terrifyingly loud in the enclosed space, echoing like claps of thunder. The holiday rep jerked backwards, blood fountaining from her chest. Johanna screamed, tugging the kids away. Dahl ran hard at the shooter, not caring for the moment whether the assailants required him alive. The cop wheeled the pistol toward him, but too late. Dahl took hold of the gun arm and shoved it up into the air. Another bullet discharged, into the ceiling. Momentarily deafened, Dahl yanked hard on the gun hand while chopping at the man's elbow, dislocating it. The cop's mouth opened in a silent cry. Dahl struck the cop in the temple with his own gun barrel. Then again. The first two strikes didn't put him out, only made him scream aloud. Dahl could have choked him into unconsciousness, but that would take too long. A third clout with the pistol butt sent the crooked cop down in a heap.

Johanna looked from Dahl to the fallen holiday rep, then back again. Fear glazed her eyes like ice on a window. "She . . ."

"I know," Dahl said, relieved that his hearing was returning. "The truth is, our fate'll be worse if we're caught."

His words, pitched low, might or might not have reached the kids' ears, but they were out of time. The cop was trying to rise from the floor; maybe had another weapon. Dahl noticed Jo's nervous glance at the gun in his hand. He caught hold of her hand and pulled them along, dashing across the nightclub floor in the direction of a pair of swing-doors at the rear. Confusion and lack of information was still on their side.

The doors led to a small kitchen and store room.

"Slow down, Torsten. We all need a rest."

Dahl choked down a curse. "Normally I'm ruled by logic and training." He pulled them toward a far door, then paused. Transferring the gun to his left hand, he bent down and picked up Julia. "But today it is all emotion."

"I don't know what you're talking about."

"Emotion." Dahl took a moment to breathe, then passed the gun across to his other hand while picking up Isabella. "It means of the half dozen or so people I trust in the world, only one of them is here, today, in this room."

"We keep running?"

"You got it."

The far door led to a narrow corridor piled high with torn open boxes, club, bar and food supplies. The team Dahl normally worked with would pluck a bottle of fine Barbadian rum and take it with them for later celebrations; he missed their presence, but to dwell on their absence would only hurt his family's chances. Emotion clouded the mind, to be sure, but it also focused it to pinpoint accuracy when those you loved stood in danger's nightmarish embrace.

A push-bar was affixed to what Dahl imagined was the outer door. Options clamored through his brain, each flawed but competing with the others. A dozen different scenarios could await them out there.

With no option, Dahl pushed gently on the pitted metal bar, cracking open the rear exit door. No alarm sounded, which was a bonus. Sunlight flooded through the gap he created, blinding for a moment. Outside, the rear of the property was bounded by a high fence and a row of leaning trees. A small area, littered with cigarette butts, food wrappers and even condoms. Bits of food rotted among the hedges. He ventured out, silent, bringing Johanna and the kids with him. They didn't stop there, but continued on, attempting the narrow walkway that passed down the side of the property. Dahl hoped it would offer an alternative way out and, in that, he was lucky. The problem was, the way out wasn't exactly civilian friendly.

A gap in the fence offered a crawlspace through rotting underbrush and piled-up litter. Dahl took a moment to review options. The only other way, ahead, lead back around to the front of the nightclub and whatever enemies had assembled there. Sooner than later, they'd be upon them.

"This is it, guys," he said equably. "Our way out of here."

Johanna eyed the gap. "Are you kidding me? You couldn't fit a dog through there."

"You could," Dahl said. "If he hunched up a bit."

To prove his point, he dropped to his knees, ignored the gravel-scrapes, and showed the kids what to do. Ideally, Johanna would go first, but his wife continued to struggle to absorb their situation.

"That poor woman," she said, unable to stop thinking about the holiday rep who'd died trying to help them. "We should go back, Torsten. The other police must be trustworthy. They can't *all* be taking bribes."

Dahl sought a way to explain how he knew what they must do. He would take any confrontation if there were the slightest chance of winning. But he'd gained a lifetime's experience through stints with Special Forces, both in Sweden and the U.S., and as with any job, a person got a feel for a situation; he knew what might work and what would definitely not work.

"I know you're a capable man," Johanna said. "I trust you. But this . . . this whole day . . ." Suddenly, she was sobbing. "It . . . it's inhuman."

Dahl compartmentalized the statement from the emotion. The statement, after all he'd gone through and terrorist plots he'd helped stop, was mildly amusing to him; the emotion needed stemming at the source. It couldn't continue if they were to survive.

"I agree," he said, putting his hands gently on her shoulders and moving closer. "It is. But there's something much more important than that at the moment. And more important than your feelings." He pointed down to where Isabella and Julia were gamely trying to fit through the small gap in the fence. "Those two."

Johanna started all at once, as if only now realizing the kids were no longer by her side. Then, without, changing expressions, she looked away from Dahl and dropped to the dirt. He had temporarily put their marital discord out of mind, but in truth such a friction could never stay far from the surface. The chances of them reconciling if they survived this madness were bordering on nil. Dahl knew danger, death and mortal struggle showed the true character inside a person. Johanna wouldn't like that he'd seen hers.

Urging his family on, he squeezed through the fence behind them, wincing as the ragged wire dug into his hips and ran down the length of his back. The ground was hard, packed dirt, and strewn with miscellaneous rubbish. The father in Dahl cringed at what his children's hands might be touching; the soldier wanted them to move along faster. It wasn't long before a gap appeared in the foliage ahead and Isabella disappeared from view. Julia followed and then Johanna. Dahl climbed out after them and looked around in surprise.

They stood on the sidewalk of a quiet street. Two-story buildings lined up opposite them, once white but now a mixture of rotted brown and other dirty colors, doors and windows standing as ragged as broken teeth. A green and yellow hut stood on a street corner to the left. A woman holding a pink umbrella strolled by, shaded from the afternoon sun. A white mini-van crawled by, and now Dahl saw another danger. People were looking at them, staring. This was the edge of Bridgetown, the capital of Barbados, and not all of its neighborhoods could be considered equal.

To put it nicely, Dahl thought.

There were tourist areas and local areas in every city around the world, and the twain rarely met. Emerging into a rough neighborhood might be a positive development, insofar as Grant would not think to look for Dahl here. Still, this was the kind of area where crime thrived, which meant that every person they encountered was a potential spotter for Grant. And whoever Grant was working for.

Dahl led his family into the closest street, figuring it would be good to put a few twists and turns between them and the nightclub, now focusing again on what might be the purpose of such an elaborate, capture-not-kill assault. Grant and he had crossed paths in the Amazon years earlier, but they'd also clashed on another, far deadlier occasion more recently. The Facilitator was so much more than what he sounded, than the image he cultivated. Truth be told, he was one of the worst human beings living in the world today.

Johanna interrupted his thoughts. "Stop!" she cried as they threaded another narrow street, the buildings becoming shabbier the farther north they went. "Just stop. I need to know what the hell's going on!"

Dahl completely understood but picked his words for the benefit of young ears. "Nick Grant. Old adversary. Clearly, he's somehow found me."

"But what did you *do* to him?"

"Um . . . crashed one of his parties in the Amazon. He . . .

lost a few men that day, as did some of his friends. That was the easy one, if I'm being honest. We met again—"

"You crashed a party?" Johanna repeated, then lowered her voice. "Drugs?"

"Nick Grant made a name for himself proving he could procure absolutely anything for a client."

"And you pissed this guy off?"

Dahl nodded, watching the street around them, getting Johanna and the girls moving again. "Twice, yeah."

"And then he shows up on our family holiday?" Julia raised her hand like a student. "Maybe he lives here?"

Dahl nodded again. "Maybe." Telling Jo that he thought he'd ID'd the guy back in Dulles airport wasn't going to help right now. "Now, watch where you're going, Julia. Turn around."

"Okay, okay." The petulant reply was part of the nine-year-old's make-up right now.

"I don't like him," Isabella spoke up. "He's a criminal." She drew the last word out as long as possible, making a big deal of it.

"How are you guys doing?" Dahl stopped with them for a moment in the shadow of a metal-roofed, windowless hut. Some kind of food stall, he guessed, currently unmanned. He held both girls at arm's length, checking their arms and legs and then recalled yet another major problem.

"Shit, we need to get clothing."

Isabella stared wide eyes as Julia clucked. "Did you just swear, Dad? Did you?"

Their spirits certainly weren't crushed, he saw. The only good news of the moment, it both elated and chilled him. They weren't close to being out of this yet. One chance encounter and their world would come crashing down. Again.

What to do? Dahl used his training, seeing it as the only

thing that could keep them going, the one thing that could ultimately save them. *Trust your training. It will see them through.*

Johanna didn't want to let go of her earlier line of questioning. "You still haven't told us who this man is and, really, why he's after you alive. I mean, he easily could have . . ." She looked at the girls and stopped herself.

Dahl could explain, but to do so would only corrupt young ears. He tried to think of the short, edited version. "Grant lays down the poison that later spreads and destroys. He's not good. You don't notice him, that's how he works. A ghost without feeling. He believes I am to blame for certain things that happened to him." He shrugged. "He may have a valid reason to hate me, yes, but only in the eyes of a madman."

"You did something to him? How bad was it?"

Dahl took three deep breaths but didn't answer. "Up ahead," he said. "One more intersection and then we'll come up with a new plan."

Johanna appeared somewhat mollified by that idea and took both girls by their hands. Dahl had to tear his mind away from how fragile his family looked, how exposed, and remain alert. He'd already seen men eyeing Johanna and her bikini; it was only a matter of time before they came across individuals who might try to take it further.

What could they do? He saw no shops for clothing, and he had no money. No proper houses in sight. No real businesses. Everything around consisted of what amounted to small, unidentifiable commercial buildings, interspersed with the occasional warehouse. No shortage of poverty. They hadn't visited the local areas the last time they came as a couple on Honeymoon. Back then it had all been vans driven to a Reggae beat, sparkling waters and vibrant nightlife. He wondered for the first time now if Johanna had been hoping to rekindle something with this particular destination. She had booked the vacation, made all the arrangements.

An unspoken statement: 'If Barbados can't save us, nothing can'.

They had to press on.

He crossed the road ahead as the sun began to wane in the sky. After three in the afternoon, he estimated. His mind sifted quickly through the day's events, dwelled on the deaths of the cops and the holiday rep.

His family paused at the next road, all eyes on him. They'd reached the intersection. Time to decide, time to choose one mortal danger from another: where to go, and what to do?

THIRTEEN

An enormous money-fueled merry-go-round was turning the cogs that ran Barbados, and Dahl wondered again if this thing went beyond the Facilitator, to another far worse entity.

Deal with what you *could* influence. Deal with the *now*.

"We need a phone." Dahl reasoned as they paused for a breather. "And somewhere safe to hide. A hotel, maybe, but even that could be risky. And a map of the area. What we have to understand is, we're on our own for some time yet, even after I make a call to people who can help us. Certainly for the rest of the day, maybe all night too. But the key thing is to get hidden and somehow make that contact."

The girls nodded, wide-eyed, likely not comprehending most of it. Johanna looked around and hugged herself close, perhaps for the first time feeling her exposure and seeing a different side to their plight. Dahl was quite grateful for her realization. Anything to give her a better perspective of what they faced.

"We can do this," he said, using his own self-confidence to bolster hers. "Believe it."

"Easy to say," she murmured.

"I know because I've done it," he said. "Many times, and much worse. Trust the soldier in me."

"I do," Johanna said, and it was clear she meant it. It was every other part of him that she had a problem with. His military work only made his other side harder to deal with.

The sound of a helicopter blasted overhead, quickly followed by its predatory shadow. Rotor wash churned down towards the streets and Dahl saw it: a black bird with silver markings, circling overhead.

"Maybe that's the news channel?" Johanna shielded her eyes, peering up. "Wouldn't they be useful?"

"Maybe," Dahl said. "But let's stay out of sight."

They flattened their bodies against the nearest wall, a flimsy sheet of corrugated steel, watching as the chopper drifted away. Dahl figured north to northeast would lead them to the center of Bridgetown, but he refused to kid himself into believing he knew anything beyond that. Instinct would find them a haven; know-how told him so.

This street was sparsely populated, as Dahl had hoped. When being hunted, it was hard to know which was better – busy or quiet zones, but Dahl tended to lean toward the latter. He led his family deeper into what had become a virtual shanty town. The condition of the scattered houses persuaded him not to chance asking for a phone, mostly because instead of giving the impression of family abodes, they reminded him of drug dens. As they traipsed through the area, Dahl beginning to notice how pink the kids' skin was starting to look, a throaty bellow ricocheted from wall to wall behind them.

"Here!"

Dahl cursed aloud and pulled his family into a headlong run. To the rear, a band of youths had filled the width of the street, bright t-shirts and tight jeans their uniform of choice. He saw no weapons, but most brandished cell phones.

Did Grant's connections reach so far and wide? If he and his family had been wearing anything other than bikinis and swim-shorts, he'd have started hunting for a tracking device, but this was an area where youths roamed free and any chance sighting might lead immediately to the wrong set of ears. Some communities were tight-knit, others stand-offish, but most passed information along at warp speed. Dahl wasted no more time wondering. They'd already traversed a fair warren and he imagined an even more convoluted array lay up ahead. At the next road, he darted right with his family. They plunged across a new road and up a sharply angled street, now in a more densely inhabited area. And higher-rent. Gates and curtained windows and peeling balconies now passed to both sides. Dahl heard the boys' pursuit grow closer. He switched quickly down a side-street, hoping to encounter the cover of a natural crowd. White walls flashed by. Another juncture and another street, heading northeast again. Johanna was breathing hard at his side, feet slapping on the sidewalk. Scattered locals were a blur as his family passed. Faces turned toward them, some closed and some wide open, many offering up confusion and surprise and perhaps even the hope of a little assistance.

Dahl wouldn't let them get involved. Civilians had already died today, cops too, and he wouldn't knowingly risk the life of another.

Unless Isabella and Julia came under direct threat.

It was only a matter of time before the boys – if they were assisting Grant – would have vehicles converging on their location. Dahl now saw the streets not as a maze, but as a trap, potentially populated by objects faster than he was. He quickly dog-legged again, heading farther east and knowing his luck would run out sooner rather than later. The children were growing tired, their legs slowing, their energy levels past spent and in need of recharging. As they raced up yet another narrow, residential street, a sight appeared that made even the confident, capable, soldier within him gasp with fear.

At his side, Johanna screamed.

Up ahead, half a dozen youths came fast, cutting them off with bottles, billy-clubs and baseball bats.

Dahl saw one chance and zipped to the side. Head down, he sprinted like a man with the Devil breathing hotly on his heels, heaving the children into his arms and turning on the speed. Animalistic yells chased him.

Stay with me, Johanna.

A low white wall revealing a garden overhung by a mostly-collapsed rear porch whipped past, followed by a surprisingly well-trimmed square patch of grass. Dahl felt every muscle brimming with adrenalin, every nerve ending on fire.

They wouldn't take his children.

He reached the end of the alley and looked back.

Johanna was nowhere to be seen.

FOURTEEN

Dahl took only a split-second to realize he was wrong.

Johanna *was* visible . . . among a crowd of youths, captive, entirely surrounded, frozen in terror as they closed around her. The scream of terror must have come when she stopped moving. Overwhelmed with anxiety for the safety of his children, he had failed to realize.

He stood now at the end of the alley, the way open ahead at another junction but now far less appealing, the gun he'd taken from the nightclub cop raised in one hand so the mob could see it as a deterrent, Isabella and Julia held back by the other. Choices darted around him like hungry birds, but every single one involved leaving his children. As he stood there, brain working overtime, a familiar face hove into view.

Nick Grant passed among the youths along with three of his black-clad mercenaries.

"Torsten," he called out in that infuriatingly sophisticated accent that didn't fit the factual man. "What to do? Torture her? Remove some bits and pieces? Lend her to the boys for an hour? Ah, choices."

"First one to touch her gets shot in the head," Dahl said. "Step back."

Grant laughed. "Wait, boys. Let's see what Mr. Dahl here suggests we do."

"What I don't understand," Dahl said, "is that I thought you were a bloody businessman, after profits, avoiding losses. That sort of thing. Not a bloodthirsty psychopath hell bent on revenge."

"Well, you would be right." Grant rearranged his jacket and tie so that they sat perfectly straight. "I am a businessman. My employer is the bloodthirsty psychopath."

"And he is . . . ?"

Grant gave a slight shrug and held his gaze.

Dahl could prolong this by recounting the events that followed the second time Grant and he had crossed paths, in hopes of infuriating Grant into making a mistake, but it was unlikely to leave Johanna unharmed. Dahl wouldn't let his wife go easily, but he couldn't retrieve her from this encounter.

"Let her go." Always worth a try.

"Oh, okay then." Grant turned theatrically to his gang of cohorts and bellowed: "Let the lady go."

A small portion of the boys gaped, but the rest stepped away. The mercenaries didn't budge. With the crowd parting, Johanna appeared in full view as if seen at the end of a tunnel, eyes red-rimmed, face a mask of terror, holding her hand across herself, the merest semblance of protection. Dahl knew women who could fight their way out of that pack in less time than it took to write down the sentence, but his wife was not one of them.

Johanna took a tentative step toward Dahl.

Grant extended a hand. "Bring those bikini strings right here, love. I'll help you out."

Dahl raised the gun and, a moment later, faced down three weapons as Grant's mercs lifted theirs. Dahl knew that Grant would belay any attack orders; he'd be worried about taking the first bullet.

"Your choice, Dahl." Grant said. "Your wife or your kids."

Dahl didn't have the bullets or the position to take them all. He lowered the weapon slightly, letting Grant know the barrel was still only a twitch away from re-sighting.

"What occurred between us, the second time . . ." Grant said slowly. "You will answer for that."

"What about your employer?" Dahl asked. "What does he want?"

"You'll see soon enough. When you all meet him."

With that, he signed to his men and the group closed up again around Johanna, her cries muted by their bulk. The Facilitator called back loudly as he walked away with his men about him.

"Come to the Jolly Roger in two hours. I'll leave tickets at the gate. I'll have somebody new to meet you there; a young lad, I'm told. We'll exchange her for you right then. Don't be late, Dahl, or you won't see her again. *Whole*, that is."

FIFTEEN

So that was Grant's game now. He wanted everything Dahl loved laid out, trussed up and squirming before him. He was that kind of a man. No doubt he also wanted Dahl to suffer in the meantime, knowing his wife waited helpless in the enemy camp. Typical Grant behavior, maximizing the hurt to feed his own gratifications. Dahl led his children away, comforting them with murmured words as they hurried through several more narrow streets in the opposite direction from Grant and his men.

He'd been given two hours. What on earth was the Jolly Roger? Where was the commercial center of Bridgetown? Embassies? Even a bloody telephone call would ease his mind. But other factors steered him away. And who the hell was this 'young lad?'

He didn't know where this meet point was or how long it would take to get there. He couldn't let Johanna down. Where could he stash the kids? *Could* he stash them safely? What would happen to them if both he and Johanna didn't return?

A plan. That's what he needed. But a solid plan could only come with a little more knowledge.

A local tended his small front garden ahead. Dahl slowed and apologized for bothering the man, then asked if he had ever head of the Jolly Roger. The man tipped the brim of his hat, grunted, and turned away, leaving Dahl no wiser. They threaded another intersection.

Isabella turned her teary face up at him. "You should *know* what the Jolly Roger is."

Dahl blinked hard. "I should?"

"Disney. It's a pirate ship."

"Ah, yes." He'd know that, of course. It just didn't fit

with Grant and the mercenary bunch he ran with. But it was a pirate ship, and Barbados lay on the eastern margin of the Caribbean. Dahl hurried the kids along, seeing taller buildings ahead, wider roads and busier streets. He estimated 30 minutes had passed since they'd lost Johanna. Isabella sobbed openly at his side, with Julia not much better, both children aware their mother was in danger and that their dad was struggling to find a way to help her. Dahl found it increasingly hard to be both soldier and father.

And husband? What about that?

No time for that. He checked for signs of pursuit, saw none, and took Isabella and Julia across a busy road — a man curiously and spectacularly alone near the heart of a bustling holidaymaker haven; a man normally able to summon one of the best combat teams on the planet but without the time or means to do so; a man who knew it would all be over before any dependable help arrived. In the end, it would all come down to choices and quick thinking.

A street performer told him all about the Jolly Roger and where to find it. The Pirate Party Cruise set sail for lunch and dinner from a dock at the end of Wharf Road. The street performer directed Dahl, then gave them the sad eyes affected by bellhops everywhere when the tip they received fell below expectations.

"Sorry," Dahl said. "No wallet."

As they walked, still wary but passing through the crowds now, Dahl allowed Isabella and Julia to slow down, then use a water fountain. Public restrooms also came in handy. No doubt he could find a way to use a phone now, but time was like a winged angel in a speeding chariot, elusive and fleeting. Memories of his second encounter with the Facilitator chipped away at his mind with knife-like edges.

The Russian *Bratva*. Fifty thousand members. A

human-trafficking operation. Why would a *mafiya* outfit like that need a man like Grant?

Dahl eyed the passing crowd as his children drank from a shiny water fountain. An odd thought occurred to him as he watched. There were no sirens on the streets, no thumping of helicopter rotors, no signs that what most people would imagine had been a terrorist attack had ever taken place. A sense of the surreal washed over him. Life bustled and rushed to left and right, every which way, individuals chasing dreams or decisions or simply each other. Could the whole episode have been quashed that quickly and completely? By whom, and how?

Dahl asked a passer-by for the time, called the kids over and started to revise his thinking about how he might save the three people he loved most in the world from the events of the next few hours.

SIXTEEN

At a fundamental level, Johanna Dahl knew exactly what she had to do to stay unharmed and alive. Foremost in her mind was the main reason to stay alive – she wanted to see her children again. To hear them laugh and succeed and play with friends. That was life – and she wanted it desperately now.

But the immediate danger of her situation consumed her whole. Surrounded by dozens of locals, herded along the sidewalk, followed by military-looking men with guns now concealed and the Englishman who commanded them all, she shrank her presence down to the smallest size possible. Fear had been the sole engineer of her capture, and she still could not summon the strength and the nerve to combat it. Large, black vehicles lined up along the curb ahead, ticking in the direct sunlight as if they'd recently been driven hard. Doors were opened, men slid inside. Johanna was pushed, prodded and manhandled into the rear seat of the last vehicle in line, a butch Range Rover Sport. Once she was inside, men flanked her to left and right, staring forward, saying nothing. The interior felt stifling until the driver switched the engine on and the air-con kicked in. Once they were in motion, Johanna's heart started to yearn even more. Every second took her further away from her children and deeper into danger. She had heard the Englishman's ultimatum and knew it was incontestable here. The fact that they'd tracked her family across half of Barbados, using cops along the way, proved it.

What she didn't know was why.

Why was all this happening to them?

Because of Torsten. That was the only answer. His

battlefield world had crashed into their family's life, and this was the result. All she knew for certain was that she had never been more scared, or in this much danger.

The Range Rover motored carefully down several streets, each as colorful as the last, until it reached a poorer area, much like the neighborhood her family had traversed less than an hour ago. Here, though, each house was gutted, its brown insides exposed, its exterior stained. The sun lost its brightness when it hit these desperate hovels, glancing off in shame rather than extending warmth. What few people populated the area turned away instinctively from the expensive machinery rumbling down their litter-strewn, pot-holed streets. Even those who sat in doorways, belongings piled at their side amid drug paraphernalia, bowed their heads.

Johanna's flesh squeaked as she shifted in the back seat, skin pulling against leather, which caused one of her guards to stare at her in amusement.

"Want me to scratch that for you?" he said, but fell silent upon receiving a hard stare in the rear-view mirror. She wanted to ask questions, to delve for information, but didn't dare. Being in the hardest, most vulnerable position of her life was entirely debilitating, and Johanna Dahl was as far out of her comfort zone as she cared to acknowledge.

Without warning, the out-of-place procession stopped and pulled over to the curb. All drivers cut their engines as if in sync. Doors started opening and one of the men opened theirs, signaling that she should follow quickly. Her second guard slid along after her, blocking any escape even if it had somehow crossed her mind. Once outside, the heat swathed her like an electric blanket. The sidewalk felt hot beneath the bare soles of her feet, making her hop a little and walk into shadow under the watchful eyes of the men.

It didn't take long for the Englishman to step up. "My name is Nick Grant. We have some time to kill," he said. "If your husband follows orders, all will be well – for you. And he's a good soldier, your husband. Always follows orders."

Johanna couldn't speak, couldn't even blink, the dryness in her mouth a patch of arid desert.

Grant nodded to the men at her side. "Bring her."

Johanna witnessed the next minute like an out-of-body experience. Out in the open, obvious in the street, a group of flak-jacketed mercenaries and hyped-up locals marshaled her through a heavy door. And though she did not see anyone in the windows or peering around corners, Johanna was certain they were being observed.

By people who had seen it all before.

Inside, the place was a wreck. A rank passageway, its floor furnished with an extra layer of grime and garbage, led past several dark rooms. Sounds came from some of them, groans, whimpers and worse. Her own room lay at the far end, windowless but at least appeared to be otherwise unoccupied. They pushed Johanna inside without ceremony, but she just managed to keep her feet. Her eyes had been adjusting for the last several minutes but the absolute darkness inside this chamber rooted her to the floor for several more. No way did she take another step until she knew exactly where she stood, and what might be lying around her.

Or creeping.

She shook the thought off, seeing it for what it was – a sneaking specter of fear. If she didn't combat it now, how would she ever survive this? How would she get back to Isabella and Julia or hope to protect them to oppose whatever future darkness came their way?

A sudden cacophony of noise made her turn around. Through her room's door, which had been left wide open, she spied a kitchen area, now lit – peeling wall cupboards, a dirty oven and a pockmarked, food-stained table. Several men sat around the table now, one of them shuffling cards on its surface while the others glugged from condensation-covered bottles. Johanna turned back to her own room, conscious that she just had time to scrutinize every inch of it while light shone in. The first thing she became aware of was dozens of discarded newspapers, piled up around her feet. The second was infinitely more terrifying – a set of manacles attached to the rear wall at waist height, proving her fears that this building served as a long-established criminal safehouse. A roll of bloody bandages lay in one corner, a broken chair in another. It occurred to Johanna that she might be able to use parts of the chair as a weapon.

Except she didn't dare try.

She jumped as a voice spoke behind her. "Not quite the Barbados Palm, Mrs. Dahl?"

She sniffed, turning to Grant. "Why are you doing this to me?"

"You mean 'to *us*', surely, since it's not all about you, dear." The cultured tones were becoming annoying. "And really, it's all about your husband, of course. Do you want to know?"

Johanna met his eyes properly for the first time. *Did she?* "I think . . . I think you people shouldn't threaten children."

"I don't recall threatening any children." Grant said. "But I do know your husband saw me back in Washington, before your flight. What do you think of that?"

He was trying to worm his way into her head, distress her with half-truths. Even if it were true, thinking about it did her no good now.

Half-illuminated by the light coming in from the

kitchen, Grant watched the emotions play out across her face. "Not now," he said. "Maybe later I'll tell you what your husband did to me. To my wife. And to my children."

Johanna tried to imagine Grant being a father to young children. Failed. She watched him walk away, wishing she had a watch. As far as she knew, they were on a countdown. Grant had given Dahl two hours. She knew the Jolly Roger, had researched it on the Barbados website before their vacation. Perhaps it wasn't far from here.

Across the hall, she saw two sharply dressed men enter the kitchen and draw Grant aside. An animated discussion followed, somewhat heated, until Grant led them away.

Left to her own devices, Johanna judged the stares of the men who sat around the table.

Some glanced at her lecherously, their feelings all too apparent. Others watched from the corners of their eyes, while another hid his face completely. Thankfully, none approached her, but at the same time, she had no opportunity for escape.

Not that she'd have dared. Pathetic as she sounded to herself, she buried the idea deep, doubting she had the courage to try, never mind the ability to succeed. *My god,* she realized, *for the first time in many months I need my husband now.*

Why had it all gone wrong? Because of the physical distance between them? The uprooting from Sweden to the United States? The long absences? As her mind wandered, protecting itself from the more immediate terror, two more suited figures passed by the door to her room, glancing only briefly inside. Neither showed any more interest but seemed entirely preoccupied with something else. More than just a simple kidnapping was going on here today, it seemed, and Johanna was quite clearly far from an essential cog in its key machinery. Minutes stretched by, each an age in which she shook, feared for her kids and watched the men play cards.

At length, Nick Grant returned. "You will be swapped for your husband at six-o-clock after two somewhat important people arrive. My employer has sent men to handle it and will be along soon afterwards himself. Your husband's fate will be far from pleasant, Mrs. Dahl, but you already knew that."

"I thought you said he'd wronged *you*."

"Ah, yes, he did. My employer promises to touch upon that when he removes your husband's right hand."

Johanna flinched, unable to lift her eyes. "I . . . I . . ." No reply could counter that. She found it hard even to think.

"And then my employer will press the point further, along with the razor blades he pushes under the nails of his remaining hand."

"Please," Johanna now said. "My children. Please don't hurt my children. I'll do anything. We'll do anything."

"Truth is, I'm not a great fan of torture," Grant said without acknowledgement. "Except in the rarest of circumstances. Your husband is that rare circumstance. One in a million. You should be proud."

Johanna couldn't be sure if he'd ignored the plea or not even heard it. The man was unhinged but intelligent, calm but psychopathic, a dangerous, toxic human cocktail.

"And so to the crux of it. Torsten Dahl is a soldier, and not a bad one by all accounts. So credit where credit is due. 'That Mad Swede,' my best contact said, 'is one serious badass. Watch out for him.'" Grant spread his arms. "I always have. I already knew. Do you know what he did to me?"

Johanna shook her head.

"I'll tell you. But first, my employer, a Mr. Vega. Now, I see that look in your eyes. You're wondering why I mentioned his name. You've watched your share of spy dramas and crime programs. You know that once names are dropped, the victim is as good as dead. Am I right?"

Johanna fought to stop the tears falling.

"Well, don't believe all you watch, my dear. Sometimes it is healthy for one to know the name of her nemesis, her husband's murderer. Sometimes it serves a better purpose for the woman to know the name of the man who sold her children into slavery."

Johanna fell to her knees, unable to process such thoughts.

"Rumors." Grant smiled. "Hearsay. Gossip. It becomes legend, myth, scary stories whispered in dark pubs and drug dens. It all helps to build the reputation of the man."

Johanna wiped her eyes.

"Gabrio Vega," said Grant. "A powerful man in a world you know nothing about. A younger Torsten Dahl killed this man's brother while interrupting a very important transaction. That day put Vega back years, though he has recovered since. I say he's recovered," Grant laughed. "Only financially. Never mentally, of course. One never recovers from the loss of a family member, eh?"

His goading made her grit her teeth until she feared they'd shatter.

"Gabrio Vega will make Dahl pay," Grant said. "Be assured. The rest of it is up to you. Come quietly. Don't make a scene. Accept your fate. Be a good girl." Grant swigged from a bottle of water and threw it at her knees, its contents spilling slowly. "Drink that. I don't want you fainting on us aboard the bloody boat. Oh, and when I say get cleaned up, you do it fast. Just remember, Johanna, it's *all* up to you."

She plucked the bottle from the ground and drank it

quickly, eyes turned back toward the card-playing men. The same men still watched her in their individual ways, while the other hid his face. Still, they laughed and smoked and argued. Drank and played cards. Time clicked away, the passing of all she held dear. As the moments drew shorter and the exchange loomed, Johanna heard an odd snippet of conversation.

Passing outside her door, a pair of new men were deep in conversation. She heard them as they walked up the passageway and as they passed by, heading toward the kitchen without glancing into her room.

"Where'll the PM be at that time?"

"At the center of the parade, giving his speech. It'll be easy."

The accents were thick with the local twang, making some of the words hard to decipher, but at the same time they sounded well-educated. A third voice added to the mix.

"It's never easy, my friend. These things are never easy to pull off."

"Oh, fuck off, mon. You know his security detail like I do. All good. This will be the start of the greatest moments of Sealy's leadership. You'll see."

"It better be. We have too much invested in this to fuck it all up today."

The trio passed out of earshot, leaving Johanna with yet another dilemma. If she didn't have enough to consider already, these men were quite possibly planning to assault the Prime Minister of Barbados. She considered what she knew. They were certainly well armed, plentiful and motivated enough to try. And it seemed likely that Grant and this Gabrio Vega were involved with the plot.

It was a shock when Grant appeared in the doorway, two objects held in one hand.

"Wash yourself off and put this on. We leave in five."

"I . . ." she managed, again forcing down the begging, the pleas and the tears. "I—"

"Save it. You already know what is required of you and what will happen to your husband. Do not make this any harder than it will already be on yourself and your children. Remember them; help them. And if in doubt . . ." he paused. "Do what I say."

Johanna nodded, swallowing the last of the bottled water and accepting a long shawl. Time was no longer sparing, vanishing at light speed.

It had run out.

SEVENTEEN

Dahl struggled with a terrible ordeal, the toughest of his life. Everything inside him, every instinct, said *no,* the risks were too great; but an equal force fought in favor of keeping Isabella and Julia at his side every step of the way.

Well, almost every step.

Starting with a look at the Jolly Roger. The pirate ship was a red-sailed party boat, upon which pirates of all ages sailed out to sea, walked the plank and swam along with whatever marine life came their way. For fair coin, of course.

Dahl got a good feel for the size and layout of the boat from seeing it at the dockside, its crew cleaning and readying the vessel for its next voyage. The decks had plenty of floor space; the benches were simple, painted red and plentiful, fixed all around. Rope swings, ladders and other tourist delights covered the double-leveled upper deck, no doubt more entertaining once the rum punch started flowing. A lower deck was only identifiable by a row of portholes. If any negotiations were going to happen, they would occur down there. He completed his recce in just a few minutes and then drew Isabella and Julia away from the dockside and the empty railings and back toward the busier areas of the town.

Could he risk the lives of his children to save his wife?

What would anyone do?

He had 30 minutes.

He tried to think like a civilian, coloring the black-and-white and occasionally gray considerations of the soldier. The attempt only made his head hurt. In the end, his soldier's body acted on its own.

As he and the girls passed through a crowd of locals and tourists, Dahl managed to pilfer a cell phone without an awful lot of hassle. Isabella looked aghast, the innocence still showing, and Julia tried to pretend shock, the veneer wearing thinner with each passing minute. Pulling his daughters into the doorway of a closed shop, Dahl pressed a memorized series of numbers and waited for someone to answer.

"Yeah?"

"It's me. Now, shut up and listen . . ."

Dahl passed every ounce of information he'd retained to a man he knew well. This person, though currently in Washington, D.C., might be able to scare up some local help, but would only do that if they trusted the help completely. Failing that, the person would head to Barbados with their team, as they would do for any comrade, 365 days a year. Dahl pocketed the phone after the call, deciding to hold on as long as he could in case his people had any news. The phone was equipped with a GPS, which he ensured was switched on.

A germ of an idea had grown to fruition in his mind. No, it wasn't perfect, not even close, but it was the best he could come up with at this moment and highly likely to keep his children safe.

Highly likely.

Dahl balked at the insufficient odds, questioned everything twice, then three times. The alternatives were far worse. He led the girls to a water fountain, stood by as they drank and cleaned, and then did the same for himself. Six-o-clock was fast approaching. The dock where the Jolly Roger sat at anchor began to fill with expectant partygoers. Dahl moved to a position from where he could watch them embark.

Isabella clutched hold of his hand. "Dad?"

"Yes?" He glanced down, a little distracted.

"Is Mommy okay?"

"Ah, yes, darling. She is."

"Can you see her?"

"No. Not yet."

"Then how do you know she's okay?"

"It's a grown-up thing. Hard to explain."

His eyes roamed the dockside, anxious to spot Nick Grant's group and assess numbers, ability and destination.

Isabella pulled at his hand again, more insistently. "How old were you when you could do it?"

"Do what?"

"The grown-up thing? How old?"

"Old," Dahl said with a faint smile, thinking of all the living his children had to do. "Very old."

"Like . . . 25 or 30?"

Julia stepped in, the big sister trying to look after her inexperienced sibling. "It's when you get married, silly. When you find somebody you love."

"Like Kristoff and Sven?"

"No. Like Kristoff and *Anna*. Remember?"

"I like Rapunzel." Isabella's mind flew off on its tangent, the conversation and questions instantly forgotten, but no doubt stored away for later when Dahl would least expect it. His heart ached for his daughters . . . and Jo.

There. He spied the gang he'd been expecting. As he'd feared, they numbered far too many to risk any kind of assault. He watched them board and tried to pinpoint where they went. It was now time to let the boat fill up and the clamor rise. He watched for a moment, then turned to the kids, fully focused.

"We will be getting on that boat soon. And then Daddy will go to get Mummy back. I won't be able to take you."

Isabella's face crumpled instantly, tears welling. Julia tried to look strong. "But who will look after us?" She knew somebody had to; it was something she'd been told in every possible nuance.

"A friend." Dahl said. "You'll be fine."

He cradled his daughters in his arms. His father once told him that no matter the journey you were embarking on, even if it was no more than a trip to the shops or heading upstairs to bed, you should always hug and tell the ones you held dearest that you loved them, because one day that hug would turn out to be your last. He held Isabella and Julia close now and didn't want to let go, never wanted to let go, fearing this was his last time. Family made you mortal. He was realizing that now.

He rose, hiding his emotions from his girls by staring up at the skies and then across at the dock. The majority of the cruisers were aboard, the line thinning out. He clasped his daughters' hands and joined the line, shuffling along until they reached the gate. He gave his name to the gatekeeper and was waved through, no emotions betrayed in the eyes of the pirate who gave them free entry. The deck rolled slightly beneath their bare feet. If Dahl had the time, he'd use this voyage to grab a few pairs of sandals and other supplies, including clothes, but six-o-clock was fast approaching and he assumed a messenger would soon be seeking his face. Quickly now, he told the kids to grab whatever food they could and sought the person he was looking for. The right person. He stayed within a crowd while Isabella and Julia ate sandwiches at his side, approaching their fingers at an alarming rate. *Thank god for all-inclusive cruises*. Nothing popped immediately but he couldn't stop looking. The examination took him to the rear of the boat, where, at last, he found just what he was looking for.

While Isabella and Julia finished their food, Dahl approached an older couple and steeled himself for the things he would have to say.

"Hi, how you doing?"

Both looked up at him, happy, faraway eyes meeting his troubled stare. The woman was golden haired and sported a necklace of pearls to match her handbag; the man wore a perpetual smile and had long since passed the point where trimming facial hair mattered anymore.

"Good. Real good," the man said. "That sky's a sight to behold, ain't it?"

Dahl turned his head, surprised. A wicked, deep red stain was spreading slowly across the horizon, more a reminder of innocent blood spilled than the dying of another day. He absorbed the sight for several seconds.

"You okay, son?"

Dahl steeled himself and got right to it. "My wife is downstairs. There are a few issues," he lowered his voice at the end of his sentence, "and the kids don't need to know." He realized how desperate he sounded when the old man's eyes grew guarded.

"Is that right?"

Dahl appealed to the female half. "Five minutes," he pleaded. They knew what he was asking, of course, and you couldn't sugar-coat something like this. It was a raw, open wound, though far from the one they thought it was.

His silent struggle didn't go unnoticed by his children. Isabella and Julia both slipped their hands into his.

The woman cleared her throat. "If we can help . . ."

The old man coughed loudly. "Mary? Maybe we should—"

"Oh, it's fine." She said. "Like I was saying—if we can help . . ." She smiled at the girls. "What are your names, sweeties?"

Dahl discarded the guilt that enveloped him like a cocoon, trusting and concentrating on the future. The father had to do his job before the soldier took charge. This was harder than fighting mercenaries on a battlefield, more grueling than any desperate knife-fight. He only had to look down into his daughters' upturned eyes to see just how hard it was going to be.

"I love you," he said, heart breaking. "And I'll be back soon."

"With Mom?" Isabella croaked.

"Yes. With Mom."

Dahl thanked the old couple and then walked away before anyone, mostly himself, could change their minds, emotions tearing a hole through every moral and unwavering belief he'd ever known. In the end, thankfully, he didn't have any time to dwell. As he cut through the laughing crowd, a face he recognized swam into focus.

Grunt.

Ahead. Nodding as he saw Dahl and pointing at a discreet door marked 'private.'

Dahl walked straight in.

EIGHTEEN

Beyond the door, a narrow staircase plunged into the heart of blackness.

"Straight down." Grant said. "I'm surprised you didn't try to gung-ho it. Big, bad soldier like you. Take us all out, eh, boat and all."

Dahl had considered it; the idea was fully within his make-up and not beyond his capabilities. In the end, it came down to categories and boxes ticked:

What were you liberating?

Who were you up against?

How many?

Who led them?

Dahl didn't need to think beyond the first to know a full-frontal assault was out of the question. Problem was, he had no real plan. Just skill, experience and a deep, all-encompassing love for his family.

He needed every ounce of concentration right now. Instant, sound evaluations were the key. The dark staircase surrendered to a widening aura of yellowish light. Dahl put bare foot after bare foot, his skin sore, his muscles aching, feet slapping against the wood with a dull wallop at each step. The deck below was narrow – a doorway stood to the right, marked 'Function room, private party.'

"Go inside. They're waiting."

Dahl entered a slender room, well-lit and clad all around with dark paneling. Benches lined the edges, none in use. Instead a motley group of men stood at the far end, arrayed around and mostly behind Johanna, who'd been given some sort of a shawl as a wrap, probably to minimize attention.

"Well," Dahl said. "You're on the right kind of ship. You

planning to hole up down here until it docks?"

His wife met his eyes, her fingers clutching the shawl around her, knuckles white.

"Don't worry," Dahl told her, moving closer. "Are you all right? Did they hurt you?"

Of course, he was playing for time while he scrutinized the space: every man, every angle, every room-based implement that he might use, including two genuine-looking pirate cutlasses attached to the wall close by the Jolly Roger's symbol.

The order of victims played out in his head. Would they consider Grant most valuable? He had moved around Dahl to stand beside Johanna. If Johanna could see it, she had a low desk to her left, the perfect place to hunker down.

"I'm fine." Johanna said. "Where are the kids?"

"I wondered that too," Grant cut in before Dahl could respond. "My guess is, close by."

"So what happens now?" asked Dahl.

Grant, the only man behind him, made a clucking noise as if considering alternatives. "Well, let me see. I think first . . . you have to meet the new players." He snapped his fingers. Three men moved aside to reveal a young lad sitting nervously atop a low stool, a brutish figure positioned beside him like a bloated, malignant shadow. The shadow whispered into the lad's ear and the lad quickly rose.

"This is Dario." Grant motioned at the lad. "Does the name ring any bells?"

Dahl thought for a moment. "No."

"Face look familiar? Come closer, Dario."

Dahl kept his eyes on the bodyguard figure, who stepped forward behind Dario. The guy wasn't for show. He looked well-muscled and knew how to handle himself.

"The lad's second name is Vega."

Dahl's awareness clicked like an electric light going on. The Amazon raid, where he'd first encountered the Facilitator . . . *and* Gabrio Vega. The drug lord had pissed himself in the face of danger, in the face of an attacking Dahl, while his brother fought back and died for it. At Dahl's hand. For his part, Gabrio Vega had managed to escape. Now it all made sense.

"Vega is your employer."

"He's been looking for you too. It may have taken a while for the stars to align, but we now have ourselves one fine cluster, don't you think?"

"Gabrio Vega sent his *son* to avenge his brother?" Dahl wondered aloud. "After all these years, the man is still chicken-shit. The worst kind of coward."

"Don't speak too soon," Grant said. "Vega's on his way."

"And you, Nick?" Dahl deliberately personalized it. "This is your revenge for the Amazon? And the Russian thing."

He felt Grant tense behind him, as he'd known he would. Dahl had been planning to use this carefully engineered moment of distraction to make a move, a well-planned but high-risk move, but Dario's bodyguard saw it coming a long way off. Before Dahl could move a single muscle, he'd raised and pointed a gun at Johanna's head.

"Not today," the bodyguard said.

"Are cheap tricks all you have?" Grant asked, emotion lowering his voice. "Then you will die. Right now. Vega sent his son to become a man, to avenge his brother. Vega sent his son to destroy your family as you destroyed his. Vin, give the boy a gun."

Dahl saw the shadow's eyes flicker at the onset of fear that abruptly froze the young man's face. With Vin caught watching Dario for a reaction, Dahl struck, tabling every hope and dream he'd ever had of the future. The closest man was a local clad in a light-green t-shirt and cut-off shorts. Dahl struck him in the chest, sending the man barreling back into Johanna and sending her stumbling toward the desk. Vin didn't look impressed, but made no move. Two more locals looked on, as if doubting their own eyes. The four mercs moved decisively, their training kicking in, lowering weapons and trying to fit around the Barbadian personnel.

Dahl went straight for the nearest gun. Vin's. He caught the gun arm and aimed it at the ceiling. Any kind of ruckus, especially a shot, might alert the right person on the Jolly Roger. Vin held steady, matching Dahl's strength. Dahl positioned Vin's body before him, so that the mercs couldn't quite reach past, the narrow room working to his advantage. When a head popped into view Dahl flicked a fist at it like a rocket-propelled hammer, drawing blood and sending its owner staggering away. Vin used the distraction to bear down on him, twisting the gun's barrel toward Dahl's skull. The man was a bull, practically unmovable. Dario shied away from it all, eyes flickering so fast they appeared to be rolling.

Trade off.

Dahl made a split-second decision to go for the slender teenager. In truth, it was perfect, the only option. Shoving Vin's arm further away he started to lunge but a blood-curdling shriek stopped him cold.

Grant. You forgot about bloody Grant!

To his right, Johanna knelt on the wooden floor, hair held fast by in Grant's left hand. Grant stood behind her, a blade held at her throat. A thin smear of blood already coated the sharp edge.

"Stand down. Or watch her die."

"Catch her from behind did you?" Dahl threw Vin's gun arm aside and moved toward Grant. "Nicky and Vega, kissing in the coward's tree."

Behind him now, Vin spoke up. "End this now. You see this man's one dangerous mother, so stop messing with him. Kill him."

Grant held Johanna so tightly she couldn't even twitch for fear that the blade would sever her carotid. The mercenaries spread out as best they could, all smiles again. The locals tried to hide expressions of distaste.

Vin draped a huge, muscled arm around Dario's shoulder, bringing the boy in close, grunting animalistic words of encouragement. With one finger he dangled the gun in front of the kid's face.

"Use this to avenge your father's brother," he said. "Do it."

Dario eyed the black steel, then the man he was being told to kill. Dahl registered every unfolding moment of it, the inevitability of death beginning to close around him. Grant watched Dario as, for the first time, Vega's son's gaze met Dahl's eyes.

"Kill him," Vin urged again, oddly gentle, much like a preschool teacher urging a child to take a developmental first step.

"You can shoot him in the leg first," Grant said, "if it helps."

Dahl watched the Facilitator in his peripheral vision. If the Englishman moved a single muscle, shifted the blade for one instant, he would make the most significant move of his life. If . . .

"Dario," Vin growled, "become a man. Shoot this soldier between the eyes so that we can start on his wife."

Dahl grated already clenched teeth.

Dario took the gun.

"And his children," Grant added. "They'll sell for more than a pretty penny at the slave market. You're making us rich, Dahl old boy."

Dario squinted his eyes nearly closed as he raised the gun.

NINETEEN

Dario's finger entered the trigger guard, the pistol shaking, then withdrew.

Vin steadied Dario's shaking gun arm. "Now is the time."

"Yeah," one of the locals laughed. "Mama's boy take a shot."

Vin turned so fast even Dahl barely saw the move. A whip-like arm shot out. The local clutched his neck, face suddenly twisted, choking. Dahl saw blood and realized Vin's hand must have held a concealed blade. Good to know. The local collapsed, still gagging. Dahl shifted a little closer to Vega's best man.

"You do not disrespect the family," Vin rasped, his voice a cheese-grater across concrete. "The family are your gods."

Dahl had been watching everyone, from Dario to the mercs to Grant, hoping for a loss of concentration. What minute losses there were offered no opportunity. He was close enough to both Grant and Johanna to make a move, but not a telling one. It began to look increasingly as if Dahl was going to have to make a last-ditch assault. His body was charged, his mind ready. Vin now clutched Dario's hand in a violent grip and aimed it dead-center at Dahl's chest.

"Pull the fucking trigger, boy."

Finally, Dario showed some spirit, pulling away from Vin and taking several deep breaths. Nobody spoke, nobody dared.

Dario aimed the gun.

Dahl gathered himself. Johanna moaned.

Then Dario turned the gun on himself.

Vin gasped out loud. Dahl couldn't wait any longer. He lunged for the Facilitator and drove a fist into his ribs, a move that would draw the blade away from his wife's throat. For a split-second, he felt a pang of hope.

Then the gunshot rang out.

One of the locals spun, dead. Then another shot and Vin fell backwards, clutching his side. Two more shots and two mercs fell. The rest stared between Vin and Dario, wondering what the hell to do.

Dario hadn't killed himself after all, Dahl now saw. Instead, he was killing the locals and mercs. Dahl pounced on the chance like a predator taking a wounded animal. Another blow and Grant was falling away from Johanna, groaning. Dahl plucked the blade from his fingers and pulled Jo close. A merc closed in behind; Dahl sent an elbow in search of the man's nose, locating it easily without looking. Dario fired again, each resounding clap making Dahl flinch instinctively. Another merc went down.

Vin was screaming at the young man. Dahl made his voice louder than the bodyguard's.

"Come on! Now!"

Dario didn't hesitate, hurdling dead men and training the gun on those who still lived. One of the mercs asked Vin if they could shoot the boy, but Vin was barely listening. The shadow was beyond livid, beyond furious.

"*He's mine.*"

Dario reached Dahl's side as Dahl broke for the far door, Johanna moving with him. They crossed the passage and pounded up the narrow wooden staircase, hearing no signs of pursuit but trusting nothing. Only Vin's vengeful roar followed them up the stairs. Dario stumbled to his knees in fear, but Dahl urged him on. The door at the top of the steps was locked, but the Mad Swede hit it like a charging bull, rotating slightly at the last moment so that his lowered shoulder struck it squarely. Hinges splintered, the lock cracked, and it surged open, slamming back against the boat's bulkhead with a resounding snap. Cheerful sounds now reached their ears, the partygoers making merry. Dahl was surprised nobody had heard the shots, but then saw a worried-looking group approaching from the ship's bow.

"Quickly," he said. "They'll take the ship back to dock. We should get lost in the commotion."

"Won't Grant's men just start shooting everyone?" Johanna asked, her voice steadier than Dahl expected.

A plausible concern.

"It's not like before," he said. "I guess they might, but last time it was all about terror. Moving people out of the way and covering tracks. This time, no one can go anywhere and their secret's already out. And look, the dock's right there."

In the fifteen minutes or so since boarding had ended, the pirate boat hadn't moved far. Dahl slammed the door shut behind them and moved away, distancing them from the area. Now Johanna clutched at his hands.

"Where are they?"

He smiled to comfort her and then eyed Dario. "We don't know each other," he told Vega's son. "But you appear to be in some deep trouble. I can't trust you yet but I'm happy to help." He paused. "If you give me the gun."

Dario let out a ragged breath, his tall, gangly frame still shaking. He proffered the gun without hesitation. "Take it. I don't want it."

"But you did know how to use it." Dahl checked for rounds, safety, and then tucked it into the waistband of his swim shorts. "Woah. That's not gonna work."

"Here. This should help." Johanna unwrapped her shawl and tied it tightly around his waist, like a belt.

"My father made me learn and prepare," Dario told them. "For a day like today. He wants me to become a man. Join the family business." He stopped in fear, casting a glance back at the door.

"Well, you did the right thing." Dahl said. "Killing is no business to be part of."

"It isn't quite so easy. I have a—"

"Torsten," Johanna interrupted. "Where *are* they?"

Dahl eyed Dario a moment more, using every minute of his decades-long experience to gauge the boy and his intentions. The initial impression was favorable.

"This way," he said.

Isabella and Julia screeched when they saw Johanna, running into their mother's arms. Johanna tried to hide the blood at her throat by kneeling and burying her head into her daughters' embrace. Dahl thanked the older couple for keeping his world safe and then turned to Dario.

"You failed your initiation."

"Oh, I know. I've known for a long time that I would. But Vin . . . he's not just a bodyguard. He's a massive bully. A born killer, but loyal. He'd kill his own mother if my father ordered it."

Dahl wondered how the boy had ended up planted so far from the rotten tree that was his father, how the genes had spliced so diversely, so far apart. He put the interrogation off for now, finding he was able to breathe the air again, see his family together again, something that had seemed unattainable only a few minutes ago. His normal self-confidence had taken a beating, but now came flooding back. Yes, he could do this. He did have the skills to save his family. Nothing had changed.

"Can you get us out of here?" asked Dario.

"I do this for a living." Dahl told him. "Just do as I say."

As the ship returned to dock, nudging the concrete

slipway, a security team stalked the deck, making the passengers bunch and lose their good cheer. Dahl, his family, and Gabrio Vega's son found adequate space in which to hide, and Dahl finally began to believe they might all survive this day intact.

TWENTY

Gabrio Vega stared out the tiny airplane window, pinching the knot of his yellow tie into a tidy bundle, a cell phone tucked beneath his chin.

"Are they talking?"

The answer came from a voice as fragile as a twig. "No. No, sir."

Vega hated to hear fear in a man's voice despite the fact that he was forced to foster it among the ranks. Goons, unfortunately, only responded to one thing, and often goons were all that was available. "Find out where they live. Use their families."

"Um, we're taking about a commissioner here. And two deputies."

"And are they sitting comfortably in your cell?"

"Yes. Yes, sir."

"Well, good. Warn them, let them go and then use the office to go to work on their families. Leave the cops alone. Start small: bank payments, car loans, alimony payments if there are any. You know. Do you understand? Use our system like you're supposed to."

Vega felt fury rise in his breast when the voice fell even lower, answering in the affirmative but clearly out of its depth.

Did he have to do everything himself?

Often, yes. Men liked this filled the ranks of his organization, but it was the shrewd psychopaths that Vega needed. People like Vin. Like Drago. But they did not come along often. He wondered if he should send Drago to Vegas. The operation there was showing signs of foundering, the competition smelling blood. That was why they'd abducted *la chota* in the first place. But physical intimidation was becoming less and less the way to go these days.

He lowered the cell phone and shouted down the aisle. "How long until we land?"

"Twenty minutes, sir."

Vega gripped the phone's plastic tightly. "Now listen, *puto*," he breathed into the mouthpiece, not enjoying the change of tactic but deeming it necessary. "You have orders. Do it now or I'll have to send Drago. Do you understand me?"

More whining.

Vega felt around on the leather seat beside him, instinctively going for his gun. It took an enormously deep breath to calm himself. The rage didn't come often these days, but when it did . . .

Don't become your own worst enemy, he told himself. A phrase from the mouth of his father, one of the few fondly remembered ones.

"Last warning. Do it. *Now.*" He killed the call, wishing it were the man, and bellowed out an order for his laptop. Twenty minutes was just enough time to start to destroy someone safely and remotely, exactly the drug he needed. And it was a drug: the need, the power to rule and kill and stomp obstacles into the ground . . . digitally. He'd once had a competitor removed literally from the face of the earth. Killed and burned him. Torn him asunder. Ground him down. Then pulverized the ashes until nothing remained. That face-to-face act brought him no kind of solace, but doing the same — via data alone — to another competitor kept him happy for months on end.

Today, though, only one thing would satisfy him. Here he was, flying toward the culmination of one of the greatest deals of his career and all he could think about was Torsten Dahl and Dario.

Did the kid come through and end Dahl?

A stab of phantom pain emanated from the old gunshot wound in his hand, the reconstructed thumb joint reminding Vega of the klutzes who worked for him and instilling in him a faint desire to be more like his father. His father would have dealt ruthlessly with such an offense. Vega forgave and laughed about it, inspiring loyalty at the same time as confusion, his men rarely knowing what to make of him.

Vega entertained a buffed-up memory for a few moments, remembering all that he had seen and conquered. It was during these sumptuous flashbacks that he felt most at ease – the jungle episode, for instance, when his brother had turned tail, shot in the back by Dahl and Gabrio Vega had fought tooth and nail through the Swede's entire crew to carve out a slice of vengeance. Only to be foiled at the last moment, as Dahl absconded on a helicopter, tail between his legs. In truth, in his most twisted, deepest heart, Vega knew this was why he hadn't pursued Dahl through the years. The memory he preferred served better than the reality he buried away.

A flight attendant paced up the aisle, smiling. Vega felt content again. Calm. The phone rang again and this time it was someone he actually wanted to speak to.

"Vin? Tell me what happened."

He sat back languorously, looking forward to hearing of Torsten Dahl's anguished final moments on earth.

"The kid shot me. Killed three others. Escaped with Dahl."

Vega's mouth actually fell open. For once, he was stuck for words, too flabbergasted to put anything coherent together.

"They made it off the boat. If you want us to find them it could . . . clash with that other business."

Vega mouthed like a goldfish, still struggling. Finally he said: "Is Grant alive?"

"*Si*. The Englisher is a cockroach. He could crawl away from anything."

"Tell him to carry out the plan without adjustment. But spread the word down there – I want Dario, Dahl and the rest of the Swede's worthless family. I want it all."

"It could deplete our cover. Cause problems."

"Don't tell me what it could do. Get it done!"

"On it."

"And listen to me. Does the kid have his tracker on?" Dario was family. Vega was technology-minded, and domineering to a fault. The Web helped him control most lives he took an interest in, but to regulate those he kept closer a different system was required. And redundancies in droves.

"He does. All three of them. Already activated."

"Good. Then don't fail again. I'll be there soon."

Vega waved the flight attendant away and started fiddling with his cell phone, turning it around and around in one hand as he decided what to do next. Three men dead – if they were his men then that meant three funerals back home, and much else to do. They might be goons, but they were his goons, and that meant treating them professionally. At least the Barbados operation remained sound. Soon, the lucrative island would fall under his control and the boost to his drug trade would be like a heroin shot in the arm – fittingly. Grant had organized the job impeccably. Vega didn't see how eliminating Dahl and his family – and now Dario – would get in the way of the mission's success.

Dario.

His son had betrayed him – betrayed his family. But he'd also killed three men and shot Vin . . .

Vega shook his head, experiencing a stab of anger mixed with guilt that felt like a sword through the heart. Who knew the boy had such a set of cojones? And who could have predicted he would use them to thwart his own father, the man who had given him a thousand chances?

Vega called home. Gomez answered the phone.

"Get me Vargas. Now."

"Yes, sir."

Forty-eight seconds later, a gruff voice echoed down the wires. "*Si, senor?*"

"The girl. Dario's girl. His little secret. You still have eyes on her." It was an expectation, not a query.

"*Si*. We do."

"I want you to do something very specific. Are you listening?"

"Go ahead."

"Cut off her head. And then send me the pictures. Do you hear?"

Vargas swallowed audibly. Vega knew it was rather an unexpected request from the boss, but this was one of those times when the psychopath had to emerge and overshadow the professional.

Vargas's answer was appropriate. "It will be done."

"Now, Vargas. Do it now."

Vega cut the connection. How did Vin come by these men? Lottery? Shortest straw? After the Barbados jaunt, it might be time to teach his business-suit wearing hoodlums the art of *listening*.

Vega looked out the window as the plane came in to land. Barbados stretched out below, sparkling from the endlessly folding sea to the roads and the beaches and luxury boats. A small tourist paradise, and a new lucrative home for Vega. Barbados was about to be brought completely under his rule. Rivers of blood would be spilled at his order.

Digital blood, naturally.

Life was good.

TWENTY ONE

Dahl, his family, and Dario made themselves among the first to disembark, escaped the dock unmolested and headed into Bridgetown, part of a swelling crowd. Sirens screamed, lurid flashing lights painting the sides of buildings red. It wouldn't do to be questioned by the cops at this point, especially carrying Dario's gun. They had also purloined several items prior to their scramble off the ship.

The kids now wore crocs, a size too small for each of them but better platforms than the soles of their sore, bare feet. They also had a short red cardigan and a thick, grey hoodie between them, the latter of which they took turns to wear as the heat of the day faded away. Johanna wore flip-flops and a knee-length cardigan draped over her shoulders, the clothing transforming her somehow into a much more confident woman. Dahl had found himself Asics trainers and a black leather jacket.

Jo had been reluctant to steal the clothing they needed.

"Our need outweighs theirs for now," he'd told her. "I promise we'll try to return the items another day."

If we survive . . . words best avoided.

Dahl checked the time by shadowing a tourist and peeking at his wristwatch. 7:00 p.m. Help remained several hours away, but now their destiny had been returned to their own hands. He pressed further into Bridgetown, seeking a special, more personal type of asylum.

As they walked, he spoke to each member of his party individually, bolstering their confidence with his own, dealing with their tiredness and fear by offering a strong, unbreakable set of shoulders.

Isabella and Julia were subdued, the day taking its toll.

Dario nodded at everything Dahl said, but the young man appeared deep in thought.

Now far from the ship, Johanna favored Dahl with a grateful smile.

"Thank you for coming to save me."

"You know me. Mad bastard."

"Sometimes mad can be a good thing."

"Did they hurt you?"

He watched his wife closely, but Johanna didn't flinch or look away. "Only here." She tapped her head. "The things they said. What they would do to you. How they would sell Iz and . . . and Ju—" A silent sob wracked her frame.

Dahl reached out to steady her. "We're almost done," he said. "The worst is over now."

"No," she said, crying. "I don't think it is. While I was — oh!"

Two faceless figures came out of nowhere, tackling Dahl and Johanna about the waist. Hitting Dahl meant his attacker met an unyielding tree stump, but Johanna sprawled and rolled across the sidewalk faster than she could cry out. Dahl hooked an arm under his assailant's body and lifted his bulk in the air. As the feet left the ground and the body tipped, Dahl let go. The man landed neck-first and went still. Dario motioned at Dahl's waistband, but Dahl shook his head. Firing a weapon now would only increase the risk. Dahl dealt his would-be captor another, decisive blow and then turned to help his wife. Isabella and Julia crouched together, faces turned away. Dario had his arms around them, instinctively moving them away from the melee. An unexpected protector.

The man who stood over Jo looked up at Dahl as he approached. Realizing he didn't stand a chance, he turned to run, but Dahl was faster, dispatching him with a single blow to the back of the neck.

He helped his wife to her feet and brought the children close with a nodded thank-you to Dario.

"You were right, Jo. Let's hurry."

They moved away quickly, escaping the stares of rubberneckers by becoming one with them. The crowds ebbed and flowed. Johanna tapped Dahl's arm.

"I overheard something," she said, sniffling. "Something really bad."

"It doesn't matter. The priority is to get you all to safety. This place isn't what it used to be, Jo."

He'd meant it as part-joke, trying to lift her spirits, but saw in her face how seriously she took his words, and how she'd been hoping for so much more from their time here.

"Let's keep walking," he said to take her mind off it all.

Johanna looked like she might capitulate, but then stopped and let it all out in a sudden surge, the floodgates of emotion opening and washing self-preservation away. "They were talking about a Prime Minister. *The* Prime Minister. Of Barbados, I think. They said he was called Sealy. And they spoke about his security detail and where he would be at a certain time. They were saying he'd be giving some kind of a speech. Maybe at a parade? They said, 'It's never easy to pull these things off.'"

Dahl mulled it over. "These people . . . were they with Grant?"

"They were meeting with him, yes."

Dahl had suspected that the Facilitator and Vega wouldn't have gathered all their considerable resources in Barbados so quickly simply to take revenge. Now he knew: they had a larger plan.

"It sounds like a hit." With back-up or even alone, Dahl would have pinpointed Grant's position and taken one more parasite out of existence; the paradox was that his family was here and he *still* wanted to snare him.

"Lucky for him, you're here. Can we call it in?"

"I have a phone, but . . ." He shrugged and surveyed the area. "Did they say which parade?"

"No. Why?" Johanna's fear grew by the second, clear on her face.

"It might give us the time-frame."

"Today," Johanna said. "They said it's today."

With that, Johanna could stand it no more, the trauma of the last several hours, the surety of her death, the pressure of right now. Her face crumpled and the sobs shook her frame. When they saw their mother sobbing, Isabella and Julia both started to cry too, right there in the center of Bridgetown, as the crowds skirted by.

We don't have time for this, Dahl thought, still in military mode, but then found his compassion as his children looked to their father for guidance. His wife tried to hug herself rather than reach out for him. He took a chance and drew her close, hoping the kids would take solace from the closeness of their parents.

Johanna sniffed. "The kids need you."

"So do you. And I need you."

"And so do your soldier buddies. And the US government. Isn't that what you once said?"

Dahl despaired then, and looked up at the Barbados skies for inspiration. *What to do now?* Darkness was a solid vault above, inscrutable and cold. He realized that Isabella and Julia had both stopped crying and he looked back down to see why.

Dario was on his knees beside the girls, speaking softly, engaging them and shifting their attentions. The young man had a good heart and cared for children. How on earth could he be the spawn of Gabrio Vega? The girls clearly felt his innate kindness, warming to him and listening. Isabella even let out a small giggle.

"Look." Dahl tapped Johanna.

She sniffled, wiped her eyes, and managed a small

smile. "Maybe someday they'll forget this."

Doubtful. "We'll do what we can." He gave her a strong hug. "You'll be okay, Jo."

"I don't care about me," she said. "I care about our kids."

Dahl nodded, hugged her again. They needed to find a place less traveled, now. Hundreds of passers-by had already noticed them. He also felt an urge to contact the incoming rescue team about the Prime Minister threat, but they were still hours away. Was this a job for the local cops? No, because the Facilitator was involved and no stone would have been left unturned, no worm left unearthed and not paid off.

Who could he trust?

Easy. The man Grant wanted to kill.

Dahl thought about that sentence, measuring its simple truth and honesty. Seven words – job done. Help the one man who could help them. Dahl had to get to the Prime Minister.

Now there's *an idea.*

He tabled it for a few minutes as he led them across the road and into the shadow of a department store, seeing it was still only early evening and wishing the small hand of the clock would start spinning a little faster. Nevertheless, he considered his plan sound. All he had to do now was locate the PM and then get close to the man. Easier said than done, especially with assassins crouching somewhere in the night, but Dahl believed he could do it.

Have to.

Grant and past memories assailed him, a constant commentary in the background of his thoughts and plans. The guilt he felt over Grant's accusations regarding the Russian *mafiya* incident was unfounded. It was misplaced, fueled by Grant's mistaken beliefs and by the suffering of innocents. The Russians had been dabbling in everything from video piracy to murder-for-hire and human trafficking. They were evil men, raised without a conscience, trained by depravity and cruelty, indoctrinated into sin by those who had been indoctrinated before them. When they branched out, they used others, partly to conceal their actions and identities but also to learn the skills of those they hired. One such man was Nick Grant, even then a procurement legend. Dahl remembered the day he'd learned the Facilitator was in league with the Russian mob, remembered his reaction.

Not a chance, he'd thought. *Grant's too savvy for that.*

Not so. The Facilitator proceeded to work for the Russians and later came to regret every single second of it.

Dahl forced it down, but it rose like bile, spilling acid into the pit of his stomach. Grant's fury would have its reckoning.

Dahl hoped for it.

TWENTY TWO

Bridgetown's shopping district bustled with life, excitement everywhere. Johanna first noted that the bustle seemed more of a festive affair – colorful costumes, face paint and the gathering of small crowds and the presence of barriers and cops– since Dahl was fully focused on keeping them safe and wondering about Prime Minister Sealy. His family had arrived yesterday, their vacation booked at short notice, and had no idea of what other events might be happening across the island. What the hell was this? From years ago he remembered watching a more authentic, cultural parade. This felt more like a politically funded affair.

As Bridgetown became an ever-growing hub for cheerful partygoers, Dahl came to the conclusion that the merriments had to be investigated. Don't leave the unknown at your back or anything past you. Well, anything that could hurt or help. The best group of people to approach appeared to be a bunch of jolly Americans, recognizable by t-shirts supporting American football teams and, mostly, by their accents.

Dahl also liked the size of their group, pulling his own among them. The first friendly face that held his gaze belonged to a middle-aged woman wearing a Harley Davidson baseball cap and short denim shorts. She gave Dahl a big smile.

"Hi there, handsome. You lookin' for someone?"

"As a matter of fact, no." Dahl grinned. "The kids were wondering what on earth was happening?"

"Ooh, you're English. Jess, Becca, listen, this man's from the UK!"

Dahl had long since given up correcting assumptions as to his birthplace. "You like the English?"

"Dunno, honey. I never really met one before. But I do love that accent."

Dahl had been hit upon many times, but not in front of his wife. The sad part was she didn't appear to even think about stepping up.

"Big party?" He steered her back around to the question.

"Kadooment." The woman said, then swigged from a bottle. "Kadooooment! They call it Crop-over too. Who knows, honey? It's all just a big party to us."

"Yeah, it's Grand Kadooooment day, baby!" one of the others cried out, then grabbed the nearest body and started to grind. Dahl winced, surreptitiously glancing at his daughters. Luckily, Dario had their attention.

Sometimes, you do find diamonds in the dirt.

He'd never heard of Grand Kadooment Day, but the first woman knew a little more. "They say it's a summer street carnival," she recited as if reading from a leaflet, "crammed with people consumed by festival fever. Soca dancing. Body paint. Just like Mardi-Gras. Oh, yeah."

"Sounds . . . cool." The family man inside him thought it actually sounded rowdy, dangerous and best avoided; the soldier saw the chance to approach Sealy and perhaps help him at the same time.

"The Prime Minister?" Johanna whispered. So she had been listening after all.

"Any celebs? Locals? VIPs?"

"Oh, gosh, not a clue. You a reporter or something?"

"Something," Dahl said. "Thanks, guys."

The crowd had thickened around them, women screeching some phrase he could not recognize. The party was clearly ramping up. Noise levels were climbing the decibel scale, gatherings at barriers becoming two or three rows thick. Dahl saw it would soon become difficult to move freely around the center of Bridgetown.

"A parade has to have a beginning and an end," he bent to speak into Johanna's ear. "The most likely points for a speech. C'mon."

They gathered the girls and Dario and extracted themselves from the crowd. Crossing over the empty roadway seemed an unnecessary risk, so Dahl headed for a cluster of well-lit nearby shops. What they really needed were some helpful locals, and Dahl hoped they might find some at work nearby. He just needed a few minutes to learn the Prime Minister's schedule and then he'd secure his family and Dario somewhere safe, allow them some much-needed time to rest.

He couldn't in good conscience allow the prime Minister of Barbados to take a hit without at least trying to warn him. It also stood to reason that the PM might be able to help them. Still, any such side benefits were immaterial – he had to try to save the man.

He stopped outside a flamboyantly painted gift shop, wondering briefly if he should take an extra five minutes to interrogate Dario. Information gleaned now could become invaluable later, but did he have the time? He placed his hand on the door handle, which pulled inward, drawing him into the shop. The girls giggled; even Johanna smiled, and the moment was gone. Inside, he spied walls hung with masks and paintings, tour guides, jigsaws, kids' accessories and a whole lot more. The woman smiling at them caught his attention. She wore a bright blue skirt and jacket, and a checkered shirt. Brighter than a sunny outlook, she saw the husband, wife and kids and began her spiel.

Dahl held up a hand. "We came out tonight without money." He grinned, unable to help himself. "Could you please tell us the parade route?"

"Independence Square to Jubilee Gardens," she said in a thick accent. "Don't go near the costume bands an' bad behave or the cops'll have your ass."

"Ah, thanks for that. I don't suppose you happen to know where the Prime Minister is speaking."

"All the talk say he at Jubilee," the woman said. "What's happening?"

"Cheers." Dahl said and headed for the door. He paused a moment, unsure where Jubilee Gardens might be, but Johanna plucked a folded pamphlet from the counter.

"These free?"

"In true."

Outside, on the street, Dahl opened the pamphlet, attempting to get his bearings from the tiny map amidst a hundred huge advertisements for helicopter rides, water slides and island cooking.

"We appear to be here," he jabbed. "Over there is Jub—"

"Want help with that?" a voice drawled.

"Here, let me take a look," another voice followed the first. "Don't wanna get lost now, do ya? Some bad areas around here."

Before the second man had finished speaking, Dahl had glanced up, recognized some of the mercenaries from earlier and a couple of luridly-dressed locals, and begun moving, pulling the kids behind him and covering Johanna, remembering the gun in his waistband and calculating how hard it would be to untie the shawl that hid it. Two men flanked them with a knotty little group behind, including the bodyguard called Vin.

Dahl saw mayhem as their only chance to escape.

But how the hell did they find us? Chance?

Doubtful. Possible, but doubtful. Faced by impossible odds, he nevertheless struck first, sending one man to his knees and the other whirling away, clutching his face. He spun and urged Isabella and Julia forward, back toward the crowd. If he could fire a shot into the air . . .

Already the men were close, though, pounding at his back. Dario went sprawling. Dahl reached down, gripped the lad's wrist and hauled him up, the movement costing him valuable moments. The jewelry Dario wore flashed under the lights, the gold watch in particular.

Obviously gifts for the seventeen-year-old. Dahl picked up the pace, an arm under each of his girls' shoulders, almost sweeping them off their feet. It was a mad, desperate run, one misstep could end in disaster for them all. It was the Mad Swede's epic obstinacy in the face of danger, his refusal to give in. Johanna, to her credit, flew along without missing a step.

They skirted a group of senior travelers, almost demolished a flower stall. They saw a cop car with lights flashing, ignored it and aimed for the thick of the crowd. They leaped over a sidewalk scribbler, decimated his onlookers, squeezed through a line of taxis. Dahl swung twice, elbows striking those who dared to venture too close. One man sprawled across the road, arms and legs wind-milling; the second only grunted and kept coming. Dahl chose this moment to wrench the shawl away from his waist and reach for the gun.

A voice rang out: "Stop right there! Police!"

Dahl didn't stop, but swiveled his head. What he saw made his heart fall. Beyond the immediate knot of pursuers, a phalanx of cops followed, weapons drawn. Onlookers were already moving away and aside and showing panic, possibly attributing the situation to the upcoming parade and Sealy's speech. Dahl didn't know, but he did see that they, a family of vacationers, could easily get disappeared tonight.

From out of the crowd ahead, four more cops emerged.

Dahl arrested their flight, hugged his children close and left the gun right where it was.

"One move," a policeman said with a wavering barrel. "One move and I will blast every one of you, right on this street."

Dahl shielded his family as best he could, but the

enemy had surrounded them, guns to all sides. The cops were working with the mercs who all worked for the Facilitator. Not *all* the cops, of course, but enough. Enough to make the difference.

"How did you find us?"

Vin made his way to the front of the pack. "We have eyes and ears everywhere. Closer than you think."

Dahl had an idea, but didn't elaborate. Best to let something slide for now that might be turned to advantage later.

"So what next?"

"Cheapside for you. And the chance to meet the man."

"Grant? Already met him. I'll pass."

"Not Grant."

Dahl's philosophy — the mandate he'd had drummed into him — had always been never to surrender. Despair clouded good judgment.

But no one who ever had their family threatened came up with that theory.

Family changed everything . . . and made the Mad Swede even more dangerous.

TWENTY THREE

Their captors ushered Dahl's party into Cheapside Market through a parking garage at its rear. The bazaar was closed for the day. Empty stalls sat in pools of darkness, and locked buildings awaited the morning and an influx of the most colorful, wide-ranging fruit and vegetable offerings in the world. Dahl and his family had been led through the streets at gunpoint, staying off the beaten track and at the heart of a twelve-man group. For passers-by, their peril would have been hard to spot. Vin stayed close but said nothing, not even to Dario. The bodyguard limped slightly, the only sign that he'd recently been shot. Dahl knew from experience the wound had to be smarting; it only substantiated his theory that Vin was the man to watch.

Dahl assessed everything, from the high access arches to the myriad merging darknesses, from the lights in nearby houses to the route they'd already covered. He watched the men around him —a combination of mercs and locals, and perceived a mix of three distinct groups of enemies. First the locals themselves, generally younger, fresher and dressed like Bajan civilians. Second, the mercs, more rugged with black coats and camo pants, most likely Grant's hires. And last, Vega's own men wearing their $1000 suits as if they were lined with gravel. He reminded himself that the hours were counting down – help would be here soon, *real* help that could take this mangy group apart faster than a Bajan merchant halved his price. But could they survive for that long? And what about poor Prime Minister Sealy? He wondered how long the man had left. Already, booming sounds of carnival and exhilaration were starting to ring outside the market like chimes of fate and destiny.

Nick Grant appeared out of the shadows like a ghoul surfacing from the darkest vault. "We meet again, my lucky friend. So tell me – how are you planning to escape this time?"

Dahl forced what he knew were haunted eyes not to flicker downwards, not to include the girls and Johanna. Grant would wring out that weakness to its most terrible finale.

"I'll let you know."

"Good. Good." The Facilitator clearly had much on his mind, as he tried to move things along quickly. "This way, guys. Try not to trip over a curb and shoot yourselves, will you?"

The odd procession moved along, passing through a series of open arches and entering a vast space under a makeshift roof. Dahl guessed this was the center of the famous indoor market, somehow commandeered by Grant.

The Facilitator's shadow paused ahead. A brief red glow betrayed the presence of other men, some drawing on cigarettes. *Quite a crowd*, Dahl thought. Only one man could command this much silent attendance.

Gabrio Vega.

Dahl steeled himself. The darkness actually helped in an odd way, keeping Isabella and Julia quiet and comparatively out of sight, enabling Johanna to range a little more freely, and emphasizing the dozens of other arches and potential escape routes that fringed the market.

All is not lost.

"Torsten Dahl. We meet again, at last."

The voice focused his attention so suddenly it felt like a nail being struck by a hammer.

"Vega," he answered. "Late to the party?"

"The men, my men, you killed needed funeral arrangements. Such things take time."

Vega sounded as if he were telling a regretful truth. Interesting . . . a cartel boss who cared about his men.

"Save yourself some more 'time' and back off."

"Ah, the dedicated, enthusiastic soldier I remember so well. This time, though, you have fewer men and I have more, yes?"

Dahl fixed on Vega as he came out of pitch darkness and into relative shadow. The suit he wore was grey and pin-striped, the tie bright yellow; lapels and knot and double-breast arranged just right. Dahl looked at the hand, wondering if it had been reconstructed.

Vega was unlike any other drug lord in the world. Impossible to read, difficult to coax into a mistake, and a strangely fascinating figure. A digital warrior and drug merchant who saw to his men's well-being.

"I could have used a man like you." Vega said. "Men like you. Vin here, he seems always to draw from the, um, denser pile, if you follow my meaning. No offense," he held up a hand to those close by. "We all are what we are."

His men nodded sagely.

Talkative, too, Dahl realized. His best play seemed to be drawing Vega into discussion, spinning it out for every extra minute possible.

"Do you have water?" he asked, knowing the question would appeal to Vega's apparently noble side. "We could all do with a drink. Especially the children."

"Of course," Vega waved and a bottle appeared. As his family passed the bottle around, Dahl watched Vega study Dario.

"What to do with you?" the cartel boss said to his son. "In a way you showed initiative. Balls, even. But—"

"He shot Vin," one of his men protested.

"Yes, yes, Mario. I know that. But Vin's been shot before. It was Dario who surprised me. And there's the dilemma."

"Well, I wouldn't hand him a loaded gun," another of Vega's hands murmured.

Vega held up a hand. "Points taken. I too do not want another funeral to arrange. How about a knife? Would that work?"

Dahl watched the crime lord and his henchmen discuss the best way to test Dario's mettle. The kid himself remained still and silent, close to Dahl, joining his protective stance in front of Iz and Julia, and taking everything in. Vega's men were bunched behind him; not a clever arrangement but a predictable one. Those Vin arrived with had dispersed around the edges of the market – far more of a threat. Dahl still had the gun and saw decent chances to grab more weapons quickly but could contrive no way to keep Johanna and the girls safe.

Vega sighed, looking at Dario, his patter finished for the moment. Dahl needed to extend the chat, if possible. Slow things down. Sometimes prolonging the inevitable led to unforeseen surprises and, currently, he could think of no safe way out of this.

Maybe they'd catch a break.

"You recovered well after the jungle incident, Gabrio."

The man froze, stared. Dahl's comment held myriad meanings and a humiliatingly deep one.

"Some men are cleverer than you think. I resurrected myself another way."

"And you flew all this way just for me?"

"Who says I came only for you? I knew you were an arrogant man by reputation, Dahl, but this . . ." He sighed again, loudly as if proving a point.

His men grunted in agreement.

Dahl cleared his throat. "Not arrogant," he said. "Confident."

"No mames, Dahl! The jungle was a long time ago. The deals you destroyed then have long since been repaired. The dead men – mourned. Now stop stalling. I have other plans tonight. It's your turn now."

Dahl made ready to attack, the soldier's brain switching on like a massive floodlight.

"And your family's," Vega added with a drop of malice.

And Dahl's floodlit readiness instantly evaporated. This day had undone him. The fear he felt for Isabella's and Julia's safety washed over every ounce of confidence he felt, every iota of skill, drowning them in a rising surge of utter dread.

Just when he needed it most, his poise vanished. Haunted, he couldn't understand and didn't know what to do.

Vega laughed into his face then, in the way of all-conquering, omnipotent men sensing weakness in his foe.

"But, Dario," he said, actually letting Dahl off the hook, surprising him. "Here we are discussing your big future without the whole picture. Forgive me, eh?"

Dahl felt more than saw Dario stiffen. Here now, he saw the *other* Vega, the demented psychopath dancing behind those clear, blue eyes.

"Who is your allegiance to, son? Is it me? My business? The men? Who?"

Dario coughed, saying nothing for a moment, but Dahl, in close proximity, knew the lad was standing taut as hide stretched over a drum. Something was happening here. Something Dahl had no awareness of.

Grant came forward, as did Vin. The three men stared hard at Dario.

"What was her name?" Grant asked. "Maria?"

Dario started as if shocked by a cattle prod.

Vin stepped into Dario's space, crowding him. "You shot me. *Me.* How easy a bitch makes you change loyalties. You remember nothing."

Vega patted Vin on the shoulder, gently moving the big man aside and back from Dahl and Dario. "We took pictures," he told his son. "Want to see?"

He held his cell phone out at arm's length and turned the screen towards Dario. Dahl saw a young woman with long black hair tied to a chair and then, as a slideshow played, the rest became unspeakable. Dario was crying, and so was Johanna, hiding the girl's eyes by burying their heads against her stomach, but even so they sensed some kind of horror had been perpetrated and began sobbing too. Johanna herself wept in silence, the terror evident upon her features, the need to live and save her girls all that mattered. Dahl saw a tiny spark in her now, something he'd been waiting for: the absolute need to protect her children, at all costs.

Vega waved the phone around, showing to his men, who displayed a mix of reactions. Dario's legs were trembling, a shock-induced reaction. Dahl used a shoulder to shore the young man up. All eyes were on them.

Dahl took a deep breath. "Talk about going over the top." He hunted for the calmer Vega with a few composed words. "Our jungle fracas isn't worth all this, Gabrio."

Vega switched his gaze to Dahl without actually seeing, then refocused again on Dario. "You die first, son," he whispered. "By the bullet. And this time there will be no getaway."

The instant he finished speaking, men surged forward. Dahl lunged alone, with no backup, Dario and Johanna frozen in terror, that spark he'd seen in her already extinguished. He punched hard, breaking a jaw and then jabbed again. Another enemy fell away, grunting in pain. Men surrounded him, grabbing shoulders and reaching for his neck. Dahl shrugged them off, swinging fists and elbows and kicking out. His attackers wailed, flinched and yelled but did not relent. Their mass was unbeatable, their commitment absolute. His arms were pinned in strong grips, his thick neck encircled by a huge arm like a boa-constrictor, allowing him barely enough air to breathe. It took six men to subdue him, but that still left more than six, plus the main players.

Dahl never stopped struggling as Dario took a blow to the head, staggering. Johanna screamed and kicked as blows rained upon her.

Then Vega's men dragged Isabella and Julia out of her arms.

Dahl had never experienced such rage. Yes, the sheer presence of the girls clouded his abilities but watching them being pulled from their mother's arms and hearing their frightened cries kick-started an adrenalin-fueled anger like none other. At first they couldn't hold him as his berserker rage powered his arms. Bodies fell away. They pummeled and kicked and scratched like boys in a schoolyard brawl, fighting to regain their grip, which they quickly did. Dahl used every ounce of strength, every hidden resource, but couldn't break free. When his muscles were sapped and the point of a sharp knife pressed against the back of his neck, he relented for a moment, willing the unaccustomed weakness to slip away.

Vega exchanged a glance with Grant, who tapped his watch. Time was pressing, it seemed. "Despite all this show, I do have other things going on tonight. Let's finish all this, shall we? Now, take this loaded gun."

Vega held the weapon out for Dario. Several men flinched away or hid behind bigger, less vigilant comrades.

Dario reached for the weapon. As he did so, Vega spoke again.

"Now, men, point your guns at the girls' heads. If Dario doesn't shoot himself in the next 20 seconds, I want you to shoot them."

TWENTY FOUR

Dahl saw Dario's turmoil, the dilemma etched deep into every feature. The gun was loaded, the faces watching him, all expectant. Vega studied his son with interest; Vin with naked contempt. Grant looked bored, clearly ready to move the night along. Dahl felt choked with emotion, every single ounce of power and strength and feeling he possessed, every iota of hope, wrapped up in the two small but immensely spirited figures now being held by Vega's men. Every nerve bled terror through his entire system.

Dahl studied Dario and then Isabella and Julia as Dario, weeping, raised the gun. His shaking hands made it hard to determine the barrel's final destination. A few grunts of warning went out, a snort of nervous laughter. Dario brought the weapon around in an arc, finishing by pointing it at his own temple.

Vega nodded. "That's right, son. Now, show me your mettle."

"Father," Dario said, "you never even knew me."

Vega inclined his head in agreement, "I require loyalty," he said. "Look at these men. That is all I need. I tried, day after day, to teach you that. When they come into the fold they are family. These men mean more to me than a worthless boy who sneaks out to go see his girlfriend and hides from his family duty. These men . . . they are of my blood. Not you. Is it the carnival noises in the distance? Do you think you will be missing out on life?"

Dario's tears flowed freely down his cheeks as the gun barrel wavered. Dahl saw his finger tighten on the trigger. Of course, Dario killing himself wouldn't change anything for Dahl's family. This merely prolonged the agony. The faces of the men holding his daughters became imprinted forever in his memory.

"He's weak," Vin growled. "He won't do it."

"You know, it's interesting." Vega turned away from his son's terror to gaze at Vin. "We have both been shot, you and I. And now I have this and you limp." He proffered a half-mangled hand.

Vin stared with lopsided uncertainty, unsure how to respond to that.

Dahl turned to Dario. "Don't do it."

"No . . . choice . . ." Dario managed.

Dahl despaired, caught between the Devil and a dozen demons.

"Come now," Vega said. "Your girl is dead. Shoot yourself. Show me how much you cared for her."

Dario screamed, his face a mask of anguish. His finger tightened.

The next few moment would live with Dahl forever, as it was one of the most shocking events of his entire life.

Johanna, until now more fearful than bold, stepped forward, catching everyone's attention. "Kill me," she said. "Kill me."

Dahl's mouth fell open. Dario paused.

Vega shook his head. "What did you say?"

"Kill me!" Johanna screamed at the cartel boss and his men. "Kill me. Not him. And spare my children!"

The balance of power shifted over to the woman. Dahl's heart pounded like a jackhammer. If anything about this day was unforeseen, it was Johanna standing her ground with such uncompromising courage. Gone was the timid nervousness. Something had developed throughout the day – a new bravery – and now she was stepping up to protect the kids before Dahl could think of what to do himself.

Dario didn't relax his trigger finger, but Grant now gave Johanna his full concentration. "You want to save people now? Show your bravery? You are different than before? Or were you hiding your true self? Women." He snorted. "A man would have to be crazy to take this one on. Are you crazy, Dahl?"

He had always been her protector. Now, she had covered for him.

"My wife is more of a man than you'll ever be, Nick. And you, Vega. I remember the jungle better than you think. And Nick? What happened between you, the Russians and your family? That's on your head, not mine."

Johanna suddenly made a lunge toward Dario. Dahl was astonished at the direction of her charge, as, it seemed, was everyone else. In the flickering dark, lit by patches of moonlight, narrow-bodied torches and the furthest fringes of pooling streetlights, disorder and misperception were Dahl's allies. Johanna went one way, away from her kids; he ripped free from his captors in the opposite direction. Grant melted into shadow. The remainder became a bellowing, human puzzle.

Johanna plowed into Dario's ribcage. The gun went off, the bullet tearing a bloody line across his cheek and vanishing into the night. Dario didn't even moan, the gun now hanging forgotten in his hand. Dahl targeted the men holding his daughters as they sought sight of Vega, unsure what to do next, all the force and intensity that had accumulated inside the suffering father suddenly unleashed. Isabella's captor jerked away as if hit by a wrecking ball, flying fully three feet before coming to earth. The goon holding Julia didn't even scream under the force of a blow that almost snapped his neck.

Dahl grabbed his daughters and moved immediately, hoping the darkness would bring at least a modicum of cover. Vega's men were about to start shooting, and it was important to evaporate, to move among them so they could not fire, to become little more than smoke. Dahl forced his girls under a stall, told them to lie flat, forced away the enormous sense of guilt he felt on leaving them, and then turned back to the battle.

Time to earn that reputation.

TWENTY FIVE

Dahl moved like a tangible patch of madness, separating men and leaving chaos in his wake. No way could he hope to defeat them all, but several new factors leaped to his aid. First, Grant had indeed disappeared, seemingly taking several men with him. Next, Vega — typically — panicked and shouted for everyone to come together. Then men began to trip over the bodies Dahl had already left behind, giving the impression that Vega's soldiers were dropping faster than a banker's promise. Finally, those who remained upright were still trying to grasp exactly what was happening.

Dahl punched and kicked and struck hard and fast, avoiding any skirmish as he circled the throng, always moving, never stopping, sidling around one enemy, progressing to the next man. As soon as a combatant became aware of Dahl's presence, Dahl tried to entangle him with the next man. He made his journey around the periphery last 20 seconds, 30, largely unseen, before Vin even came close to regaining control over his crew. Handguns were waving in all directions, even toward Vin and Vega. Some men thought the departed Grant was Dahl and fired in that direction. The shots rang out clear and resounding, and would draw the police, even beyond those already present.

Last Dahl had seen, Johanna and Dario had slipped out of sight, under a stall. He caught hold of another man's jacket and pulled him sharply off-balance, forcing him against the next who stumbled and dropped his weapon. Cries of derision broke out. Dahl skipped around the group, then punched out at the only man who saw him, sending him to his knees. Now more heads swiveled, eyes seeking, and Dahl saw that his few moments of free license were well and truly up.

Two gunshots rang out. Dahl saw men duck, but he knew Dario had fired into the air. He could see the boy's head peering out over the top of the stall where Dahl had stashed the kids. Now was the time. A vast advantage had to be taken from the lack of visibility, the endless, winding hiding places and escape routes, and the level of chaos they had engineered. Thanks to Johanna's new bravery and Dario's ongoing aid, they had somehow contrived an escape route.

Dahl placed his future firmly before him and went for it.

TWENTY SIX

Dahl came from behind Vin, believing he had him unawares, but the large bodyguard was ready, rolling at the last moment and sending Dahl flying. Dahl sprawled headlong, but was swift to roll and recover, ready for Vin as the bodyguard descended with a jabbing blade.

Dahl caught the wrist and held tight. The blade stopped in mid-air, four inches from Dahl's left eye, tremoring with the strain of their struggle.

"Grant and I," Vin whispered. "We have a deal."

"I hope is has nothing to do with wrestling and baby oil," Dahl breathed, trying to inject a little looseness into the tense situation but failing under the bigger man's brute force.

Vin bore down relentlessly. "No, with your pretty daughters. We're gonna sell them and split the profit."

Dahl compressed his body to the side, feeling rough asphalt scrape away flesh but ignoring it, slipping out from beneath Vin and letting the blade drive harmlessly, point-first into the macadam. From his knees, Dahl delivered two lightning punches, but Vin barely moved. The next struck the large man's temple. Vin grunted. Dahl rose and kicked the man away so that a gap opened up between them.

Only a handful of seconds had passed since they'd come together. Vega was bellowing somewhere, his men casting around with their pinprick flashlights. Shots rang out, but Vega yelled sarcastically at someone to *stop shooting at the fucking moon!*

"I don't think he's happy with your choice of men," Dahl said.

Vin lowered his head and tackled Dahl hard around the

waist. Dahl was strong enough to hold his ground, much to Vin's surprise. Dahl smashed elbows down upon the man's back, then punched in from both sides. Vin pulled back, but Dahl wouldn't let him go so easily. Two more blows to the side of Vin's head sent the bodyguard reeling back.

At that moment, the two men Vin had been leading, who'd ranged ahead unaware of the melee behind them, materialized like Halloween ghosts popping up out of the gloom, one of them holding a gun at arm's length. Dahl immediately pulverized him, not standing on ceremony nor even acknowledging the weapon. It was sometimes better to act without hesitation than allow a situation to take shape. The other man saw his chance and hit him hard.

Vin had recovered. "No way out," said the bodyguard. "Not this time."

Dahl throat-punched the second ghost, but Vin was upon him, first ramming him, then staggering Dahl with blows as he tried to recover.

Dahl went to one knee, heart on fire, limbs leaden and screaming, but that single, desperate, horrified voice inside spoke for his children, bawling and hollering and spurring him on. He caught Vin's roundhouse kick and heaved the man away, gaining a fraction of a second's respite.

A shot rang out, then another. Vin paused, then stared stunned down at the two red spots that began to bloom across the white shirt that stretched across his chest.

Then he looked up, mouth falling open. "You?" he gasped. "Again?"

Dario stood behind his bodyguard, pistol still pointed at the big man's torso. The youth had shot his mentor again, and this time his enemy wasn't coming back.

Vin collapsed, a pool of blood forming quickly around

him on the street. Dahl quickly finished off the other two men so Dario wouldn't have to step up again, then rifled through Vin's clothing for a gun.

"Why didn't you shoot him?" Johanna wondered, peering up from under the table and looking a little confused.

The British phrase *my head's a shed* didn't do her question justice. How could he tell her that in any other situation he'd have taken a gun and dispatched Vin from behind in less time than it took to blink? That, if you started with two-parts danger and then added family to the mix all you ended up with was a blend of second-guessing and low confidence and a head full of churning blades – each a conflicting thought whipping from side to side?

"I . . . wasn't thinking right." He breathed, but then reached out a hand to his wife and children. "What you did, Jo," he said. "Was brave beyond belief. I—"

Dario spun. "We have to run." And I need one of these guys' shirts."

Of course, their pursuers wouldn't stop. They would be ranging out now, aiming torches in the direction of the gunfire and striding toward the spot. Vega would be among them – Dahl couldn't see any figures; they were too far away – but there was no way he'd let this lie now.

Couldn't I just track him and shoot him now? End all this?

But it wouldn't end. There was more at stake tonight than Dahl and his family. Nick Grant was also at large. Killing Vega wouldn't save the PM or his family, though he'd take the opportunity if it presented itself. In truth, he needed to know what they were really up to.

The Swede pulled it together. Ordinarily, decision making and self-esteem were no problem for him. Today, his outlook had changed. He coaxed Isabella and Julia

135

from under the table and then led the way towards the farthest, darkest point, moving steadily and keeping to the shadows. They made no sound, even Johanna staying calm, focused and understanding that only complete silence would keep them alive. No tears lined her face and Dahl saw a simmering new fire present in her eyes. If it was at all possible this woman would keep her children alive.

They flitted to and fro, unsure if Vega had positioned men around the area, seeing the streets and roads that led to safety but skeptical that they could make it to Jubilee Gardens by using them. Somewhere, possibly ahead at the fringes of the parade, Vega was audibly becoming more and more angry and then Dahl heard the shout of an unhappy man.

"Damn!" Vega cursed. "Damn you Dahl! I will find you and I will rip you to shreds. You hear me? I'll be back soon. You fucking hear me?"

Dahl led his family away from the darkness and into the night.

Dahl, alone, considered every option. Some time had passed since he last saw his family, and the separation, not to mention the actual parting, weighed like granite anchors upon his heart and soul, but the distance had become necessary.

He worked his way carefully toward Grant and his men now, feeling both pleased and miserable. When he initially realized it was essential that he double back and at least try to become privy to Grant's plan, the idea had lured out a tangled sense of dread. Leave Johanna and the kids alone? Here . . . now. But they had two guns and the advantage of concealment. And they also had Dario.

Dahl didn't like it though. The kid had shown that he cared, had proven his bravery and had nothing left to lose. Dahl had faith in him to a certain extent.

"Can I trust you with this?" He'd spoken quietly to the younger Vega at first.

"I will stay with them. I will protect them with my life if I have to."

"Why? Why not run?"

"Because they are *children* and should not have to endure this."

A man after his own heart, Dario impressed Dahl. "I agree. But this is my family. My whole world. Today, they confound me and tomorrow they will astound me. Nothing matters without them."

"I get that." Dario had said. "I truly do."

And the Swede believed him. Despite his youth, and perhaps because of the peculiarities of his father, Dario had found something deep with Maria that had now been torn asunder. He was a boy floundering in a storm, searching for shelter.

Dahl offered refuge. "I have to find out what they're planning. Look after them. I'll be back in a quarter of an hour."

Dario looked relieved. "Yes. I can do that."

Dahl then moved on to Johanna. The same request should have been met with protest, with self-righteousness, with tears perhaps, but his wife remained stoic, listening to the argument and then simply promised to take care of the kids.

Dahl had studied her, amazed. "Did I ever really know you?"

"Of course. But sometimes . . . we grow."

He'd nodded. "I guess."

"Go do your job." Johanna had leaned in to deliver a goodbye peck on the cheek. "And don't worry. We'll all be here when you get back."

Running in tandem with his need to help Sealy was the

knowledge that the Prime Minister would then help them, and this nightmare would be over. The risk was worth the payoff. The paradox came in the form of eight- and nine-year-old girls. It turned good sense onto its head. Life had never thrummed with this much ambiguity.

He reviewed the conversation and the change in Johanna as he returned to them now. His wife hadn't changed – she had grown. He needed her now as much as he ever had, as much as the first moment he knew that he loved her. Everything that had passed since – surges of life replete with incredible highs and lows – was just filler. The true foundation hadn't crumbled. He knew it was simply, in the course of life, you *forgot* you needed each other. Living intervened. Complacency took root and you forgot the great things that drew you together in the first place. Children came along, higher priorities, no privacy. Problems escalated and extended like rotten, blackened roots, looking to spread and poison the whole tree.

Behind it all, if you could find it, that initial spark, the fire that started it all, never extinguished. He stopped now, in the dark, mind clearer. The twenty minutes he'd been away had helped make a sharper focus of the jumble, sort the soldier from the father. He'd earlier decided to risk it all to stay alive today. Johanna's attempt at the ultimate sacrifice had pushed her closer to his world. Now, they would have to grow closer still.

TWENTY SEVEN

Gabrio Vega had experienced a rare moment of clarity when he realized Torsten Dahl escaped. He stared around at his men – each a muscled, tattooed thug dressed up in a $1,000 suit. He looked down at himself and the weak hand that hurt every time he grasped something wrong or went out into the cold. He reviewed the years of Dario's childhood – his growth into a young man – and considered for once that maybe it wasn't all the kid's mother's fault. Mostly, though, he recalled that jungle clearing.

You pissed yourself, then ran like a coward. Dahl saw it all but said nothing today, probably hoping silence might save his children. It's true . . . you blame him for so much more than the death of your brother.

Clarity stung like a metal-tipped lash, razor-edges reopening old wounds. The gates of Hell beckoned but it was simply a lost kingdom now, yawning and swallowing up one and all . . . except him. Never him. These men – *his* men – knew from day one that they stood in harm's way. He always believed that the level of loyalty he offered, not threats, kept them together, true brothers in arms, his world a bazaar of madness with eddies of safety, of chaos counterbalanced by comradeship and care. He stood, a figurehead, at the tip of all that, a benevolent father.

Where did all that leave him now?

On the edge of . . .

"Gabrio," a familiar voice spoke near to him. "It really is now or never. The PM's on his way. We catch Dahl later."

Vega exploded with a kind of verbal madness, screaming after Dahl, and then calmed himself and ensured that his men were carrying their fallen fellows to an agreed pick-up point. His mind then switched again, this time reluctantly leaving the whole Dahl situation behind and focusing on the whole reason for him being here tonight. This night, of all nights.

"Are we ready?"

"We are," the Facilitator said. "Physically and digitally."

Vega knew certain alpha-numeric strings had to be pulled at his facility back home to smooth the process here in Barbados tonight. Of course, if he didn't have to be here right now, he'd have been tucked in there instead, tequila in hand, music surrounding him, keeping his mind clear so that he could design the tip of the computer-generated phalanx that would penetrate the defenses of his enemy.

"How long?"

"We should move."

Grant turned away. Vega looked to his men, nodded at one's suit so that the man knew to brush off a few specks of blood and at another to straighten his tie. When he caught up to Grant, he found himself wanting to explain.

"I so wanted Dario to succeed," he said. "The need blinded me."

"He's your son." Grant said simply.

"Not anymore." Vega said. "Not after we hurt Maria."

"You think?" Grant shot back, then amended his tone. "Do you regret that now?"

Vega didn't know. "It showed that my men are loyal. They deserve the same in return."

Grant led the way, steering them east along Cheapside Road, further and further under the umbrella of noise that accompanied the Grand Kadooment Festival. Vega shouted orders to his men, showing a rare display of anxiety on his part, attempting to bring them into line for what had been seen for some time now as one of the pivotal nights of Vega's leadership – its climatic events catapulting them all into a far higher stratosphere.

"This next step will bring unbelievable heat down on you," the Facilitator said. "And in the end, if they really want you, they can always get to you."

"I know that. The Americans make no bones about it."

"Then you're quite ready?"

"I do have other mediators," Vega said. "Apart from you. Don't worry yourself, Grant. The plans are all set."

Grant stopped and then pointed toward the end of the passage where the covering darkness offered by the narrow alley ended and a bright ribbon of color passed before them.

"Then let's go make history, old boy."

TWENTY EIGHT

Grant and Vega had led the way back to Bridgetown. When Dahl had left to find them, he'd known it would be a struggle to get close, but managed to quickly swing around the market and make off with a jacket and beanie hat worn by a dead thug, a local man Vega hadn't considered one of his crew and therefore not worthy of burial. It was easy bypassing the men carrying their dead comrades – they had bigger concerns than a flitting shadow – and in any case they fell behind presumably to await the arrival of one of the Range Rovers. Dahl then joined the ranks of Vega's bruised security detail, assisted by the utter darkness of the alleyways they stalked through, the woolen hat he'd managed to cram down over his more striking features and the shirt he'd stolen from the dead man. Walking with a hunch rounded it out, but it was far from perfect and Dahl wished there were another way.

But since he was already here . . . who knew what useful tidbits he might learn?

"The plans are all set," Dahl strained to hear Vega say.

Grant replied, but Dahl missed it. Cursing in silence, he inched as close as he dared as the group converged on the alleyway's exit. A few more choice snippets of conversation lightly massaged his eardrums.

"We'll have to get a move on." Grant urging Vega.

So he had no precise schedule, but the appointed moment was fast approaching.

"Where does this come out? Jubilee Gardens? Good, that's close enough."

And a place.

"We'll see Sealy there, right as he's speaking."

Dahl had heard enough. Whatever Johanna overheard earlier was about to come to pass and Vega's crew were primed and ready to act. Every moment he wasted following these men now put Sealy's life in further danger. Still, he would not leave his family wondering. He would return and re-join them, keep them close. The size and exuberance of the parade almost guaranteed anonymity, which was why Grant chose it, of course. But what worked for the killer would work for the victims too. And the rescuers. He slipped back and away from the group, retracing his steps.

The memory of Johanna and her new bravery rode shotgun in his mind, demanding attention. In comparison, his own abilities and self-confidence were twisted beyond recognition by the accompaniment of family. Dahl did not recognize the man who fought today, but knew if he could get Jo and Iz and Jules to safety, then the real warrior would resurface and quite likely save the day.

Logic, not ruled by emotion. Based on experience.

Dahl crouched low to find the gap in a fence behind which Dario and his family were hidden. He whistled the Hunger Games' mockingjay tune, pitched low, to signal his return. He squeezed through the fence.

"We have to go now, guys. We have no time. PM's in big trouble. Stick together and follow me."

A rapid scan of faces assured him the adults were assured and ready. He hated having to bring Isabella and Julia along, but the alternatives were worse. Again, the huge parade would serve them well.

"No cops?" Johanna asked.

"None I've seen. And none we can take a risk on."

"So you intend to get as close as possible to the Prime Minister, who's about to be assassinated?" Johanna pointed out as they walked. "That sounds a little mad, Torsten."

"I am mad, Johanna. It's why you married me."

They'd originally met as schoolkids, chasing an imaginary monster through the woods that backed onto their homes. Dahl had organized the neighborhood children into groups, given them specific jobs to do, and handed out backpacks, water flasks and packets of sandwiches, assuring their mothers they were going 'fishing.' And they *were* fishing – only not for fish.

Their friends, one by one, had given up and gone home, until only Johanna and he hunted in the forest. And she'd believed him when, later that day, he said he'd spotted the enormous, stalking furball. Together they'd charged at the unknown, sharpened sticks raised high.

"I remember," said Johanna.

They found no prey, no threat, in the forest that day; no danger greater than a fourteen-year-old boy's imagination. But they had been mad for a day and loved it. Dahl had been mad for years. Everyone told him so.

As the group moved ahead, a tiny voice spoke up. "Daddy?" she said. "Daddy, can we go home now?"

And walls came crashing down. Perspectives crumbled. The world contracted instantly to a very different place. It took every last ounce of commitment to stay on the path he'd chosen.

"Soon, darling," he whispered. He wanted to sit his daughters down, listen to them talk, hold them and at least try to explain.

"One day you'll understand why we can't go home right now," Johanna spoke for him. "For now, you have to be brave, okay?"

Dahl led them on, keeping his face to the shadows.

TWENTY NINE

He knew how to save Prime Minister Sealy – a stranger, a man he'd never knew existed before today, not even by name. Dahl could save his life. Spurred on by engrained principles and no small commitment to his soldier's sense of honor, he clung hard to his decision. The dilemma was he'd have to get close enough to personally attack Sealy in order to save his life. There really was no other way. As plans went, it was pretty simple and, in the past, it was the simple ones that always worked best.

Dahl mulled that over now as he led the way. Up ahead, the carnival procession twisted by, and they quickly approached the noisy intersection. The pitch-black, silent skies above played dark gooseberry to the flamboyant colors and intense noise below. Despite everything, Dahl stopped to take it all in as they emerged from the side street, astounded by the breadth of the parade. Women dressed in homemade, vibrant bikinis made up the majority of the marchers, at least as far as Dahl could see. Hundreds of figures filled just this section of the street, and the parade vanished into the distance, both to the back and at the front. A few vehicles rolled slowly through the midst of the procession, trucks with billboards and dancers aboard. Ten deep, they laughed and capered around and sang to one another. They shook musical instruments and banged on drums. They mingled and boogied and twirled to the vivid beat, a rich and multi-colored street party snaking slowly down Lower Broad Street. Onlookers and tourists lined up behind dour-green barriers, waving their arms in time to the music or cheering on certain antics. The noise swelled around the street, augmented by the high-walled buildings, and mushroomed toward the skies, a distended bubble of festive abandon.

"Oh, wow," Julia said, thoughts of home momentarily forgotten. "This is amazing."

Dahl agreed, but aimed for the narrow path behind onlookers that uniformed officials kept clear. They made good time, ignoring the parade and following a circuit toward Jubilee Gardens. A towering palm tree stood ahead, one of the signature markers of the gardens, but Dahl simply followed the signs. Soon, he made out a yellow-painted building and a noisy, bustling crowd – not a row of onlookers but a proper, dense throng. At its head, Dahl knew, Prime Minister Sealy would stand.

They hurried along, Dahl guiding Johanna and the children through the crowd. He asked them to bow their heads, and Johanna to tie her hair into a bun. Anything to keep the disguise in place.

Dahl skirted the crowd until he reached its front. Jubilee Gardens was a relatively small, mostly paved area without fences, so the people ranged out into the road. A few buildings bordered the street and the ocean could be heard but not seen in the near distance. Dahl saw several pinprick lights and guessed they belonged to sailing ships. It felt like days had passed since they made their headlong dash down the beach, onto the small watercraft, and into the sea.

He beckoned everyone together. "This is as close as you go." He paused as the crowd began to quiet, heart beating faster as he realized the appearance of Sealy was imminent.

"I want you to meet me at the tall palm tree. Stay there. Give me time, but if Sealy goes down and I don't appear, you get the hell out of here. Understand?"

Dario nodded, but Johanna was far from convinced. "I'm coming too," she said, turning his expectations upside-down once again. "You shouldn't do this alone."

"They need you more." He said, indicating the children. "They can't be without both their parents, Jo."

The crowd hushed.

Dahl fought the desperate urge to hug Isabella and Julia, to feel their untainted spirit enfold him one last time before leaving. He did touch Johanna on the hand and felt her fingers close upon his own.

"Be safe."

"I will. And, Dario. Look after them."

Overlooking the incongruities raised by speaking those words to Vega's son, Dahl hustled away, urging his burly body through the crowd. He threaded towards where he anticipated Sealy would appear, easing men and women aside without too much hassle. No sign of Grant, Vega or any of the cartel boss's men. Police were everywhere, arrayed in front of the crowd and throughout. Dahl anticipated several problems to his approach but wasn't about to stop now. Half way through he slowed as cheers erupted and the man of the hour appeared.

"Sea-ly! Sea-ly!"

The PM had certainly brought his fan club. Dahl parted the throng a little more forcefully, now only three rows from the front. Arms and shoulders and hips bustled him, the crowd denser here, slowing his progress. Sealy appeared ahead after climbing some unseen podium, raising his arms and basking in the limelight.

Dahl cringed inwardly, seeing the perfect opportunity for a gunman to take a shot. As he pushed through the last two lines, Sealy started to speak. Dahl inched along the front of the line, between two policemen and closer to the Prime Minister.

One glance at the podium revealed the depth of his problem.

Two bodyguards flanked the raised dais, one on each

side. A third stood in front, directly before Dahl. What appeared to be a fourth waited toward the rear, possibly a spotter and a man who would lead the way if the PM were forced to flee the area.

"Welcome to Grand Kadooment Day!" Sealy began.

The crowd roared its approval, and chants of "Sea-ly" began anew.

Dahl assessed the setting, seeing the potential for utter chaos and easy assassination. No wonder Grant had chosen this moment. The Bajans were in their element, jovial and all guards down on such a merry day. He moved a little closer.

One distraction . . . just one. He realized it was unrealistic to wish for some kind of disturbance to help prevent an assassination. Second after precious second ticked by and Dahl knew he couldn't wait a moment longer.

It's now or never. You're lucky they waited this long.

Gathering his wits, Dahl sprang forward like a man leaping for something unreachable.

THIRTY

Dahl came to a sudden halt, stopped bodily by one of the prime minister's own men. The man was broad and dense, a body-builder with a neck as wide and wrinkled as the trunk of a palm tree.

"I need to speak to Sealy," Dahl said with as much authority as he could muster. "Now."

"Go, before I have you arrested."

"You don't understand."

Dahl tried to squeeze past the man, expecting at any moment to hear that fateful shot. Sealy stood up high, a clear line-of-sight all across the gardens.

"Don't make me hurt you," the man growled.

Dahl stood back, unable to keep the surprise off his face. "Now that's an ambitious thought," he said. "But hardly probable."

The guard grunted and grabbed him around the waist, muscles bulging. Dahl sighed and maneuvered the man around, trying not to break anything as he flipped him onto his back. The air whooshed out of him with an *ooof*! Dahl stepped over the fallen protector, knowing he'd been seen by the other guard, a cop and dozens of whooping spectators.

Playing the would-be assassin after all, then . . .

Sealy continued speaking to the crowd, a vast curve of darkness stretching above him. Dahl vaulted onto the dais that supported the podium and came face to face with a gun.

Held by the second guard and pointed straight at his face.

"Come on!" Dahl cried, frustrated. "I'm trying to save your boss. Please, put it down, mate."

149

"On your knees," the guard said simply.

Dahl saw Sealy looking across and down, now, interrupting his speech. It became clear that it was now or never, in more ways than one. He crouched as if complying, then used the position to spring up, grab the gun arm and head-butt the guard to the ground. Blood sprayed but Dahl had no choice; the guard would be okay in an hour or two. Another few steps and he was shouting in the face of Prime Minister Sealy.

"I work for the US government," he said. "There's a threat on your life. An assassin. You have to take cover."

Sealy was an older man with thin-rimmed glasses and a light dusting of grey in the small patch of black, curly hair that tried in vain to cover the top of his skull. The eyes behind the glasses were piercing and small, and now they bored into Dahl.

Sealy said nothing. His men were closing in, yelling.

Grant and Vega's assassin would surely be on tenterhooks now. Why hadn't they fired?

"They're gonna shoot you!" Dahl cried.

A man tackled him, but Dahl withstood the charge, shrugging him off, wavering only slightly, like an oak tree in a raging hurricane. The crowd were screaming at him, some running forward with arms upraised and fists shaking. The cops were converging. Those spectators behind the front row were also breaking ranks, coming forward. Dahl saw this entire situation becoming more fraught with danger as each second passed. More than one man might die now.

"Just get down."

He reached out both hands and planted them on the shocked Prime Minister's shoulders. The face glared at him, the eyes narrowed. Not a hint of shock or surprise furrowed the mature features. Dahl experienced a stunning light-bulb moment, the reality of it all hitting him like a bolt of lightning.

"You're not the target," Dahl breathed. "You're the fucking *client.*"

Dahl backed away, limbs drained of all energy and brain reeling as if hit by a train. Sealy had been the PM of Barbados for many years. He'd been *put in place* by the bloody cartel. Something else was going down. Something that required the presence of the man who ruled this realm – Gabrio Vega.

Dahl fell back off the platform, dazed as bodies surrounded him, some pummeling, some shouting, but all he saw through the haze was Prime Minister Sealy staring down at him, a smug smile on his dark face, those pinhole eyes glinting behind their glass shields.

I tried . . . tried to do the right thing . . . risked my family to do it. And now . . . ?

He'd been rewarded with a glimpse into the face of the devil himself.

Dahl became aware again of his immediate surroundings. The reaching arms, the angry faces, the spittle-flecked lips. He heard rather than saw the unleashed energy of the crowd as they erupted with every emotion from fear to joy to fury. Sealy turned away, attempting to calm the storm. Dahl rolled and kicked and tried to scramble to his knees but knew full well he was going nowhere.

"Hold the bastard down," someone said. "Let me get a set of cuffs on him."

What's the plan for Barbados, then? Dahl thought. *What are Vega and Grant doing here?*

"Shoot him," someone else said. "Belly shot. That'll take the starch outta him."

The shot rang out. Dahl flinched, awaiting the pain, but instead he took in the looks on the faces of those who surrounded him, their expressions transforming through several odd stages, ending in confusion. Another shot rang out. Men jumped away and checked on Sealy. The PM was already hastening down the podium steps, searching for guards, not even glancing toward the struggle around Dahl.

Screams split the night. The bodies around him suddenly receded, and he saw stars again, real stars that shone in the night sky. Most of the men surrounding him ran; others stood in bewilderment. Dahl nursed one hopeful, wonderful thought:

Dario.

From experience, he knew the shot had come from a pistol, likely the same make of gun as the one Dario held. Probably fired into the air, much as the boy had done at the market. Although nothing was certain.

Still surrounded, Dahl rolled now, smashing legs aside like pins being by a bowling ball, rising to his feet as men fell all around him. A cop with flinty eyes moved toward him. Dahl ran in the opposite direction, confident he wouldn't be shot amidst so many innocent bodies, and grabbed his first real view of the scene.

Jubilee Gardens was in uproar, reminiscent of a few battlefields Dahl had seen in his time but minus the violence and death. Civilians in colorful clothing fled rapidly in all directions, filling the road and the streets and the fronts of buildings, streaming toward the ocean, hunkering down behind parked calls and walls. Palm trees shook with the passing hordes. Dahl spotted exactly what he wanted to see by the big palm and then jumped high and far, off the stage, like the lead singer of a rock band leaping into his adoring audience.

Except Dahl landed on his feet.

And ran for his life.

THIRTY ONE

Dahl made a bee-line for his family and the enormous palm tree, which offered meager shelter from the stampeding crowd. More than one man was bowled over by Dahl, but he took care to skip around older folks and those with kids. Suddenly, a shocking force struck him from behind, bearing him down, but Dahl fought back and managed to keep his feet. His head whipped around to see the steely-eyed policeman hanging on to his shirt, ripping it at the seams. Dahl threw an elbow back, blackening his eye but the plucky cop held on. Dahl stopped suddenly, let the cop's momentum carry him past and then helped with a little roll of the shoulders. The cop left the ground, breath taken away, and landed hard. Dahl felt sorry for the man – seemingly an innocent – but he knew time was as important now as it had been ten minutes ago. Actually, their situation had grown worse.

Dario met him. "Are you all right? What went wrong?"

Dahl enfolded his family in his arms. "Was that you?"

"Yes. Everything fell apart and we lost you. It was all I could think of."

"Well, I think you saved my life." Dahl allowed a half-smile. "But we have to get away from here."

He moved even as Dario and Johanna quizzed him, trying to stay hidden within the crowd, which was finally starting to disperse. Ambulances were arriving to join the few that had already been stationed around the garden, but Dahl didn't see anyone badly hurt, just a few scrapes and bruises.

"We're going to have to rethink this whole thing."

"What happened up there?" Johanna asked again.

Dahl ducked past a dozen-strong group of escaping tourists, pulling the others along. "Sealy's a bad egg." He said. "Not a target. I'm guessing he's part of Grant's network. One of Vega's cronies."

Johanna blinked rapidly, mouth falling open with naïve misunderstanding. "But he's the Prime Minister of Barbados."

Dahl murmured an affirmation. "He was furious to see me up there. Happy to see me taken down. Believe me, Jo, he's in on this."

Dario asked the prize-winning question. "So, what is *this*?"

"I don't know," Dahl piloted his family around another group of stragglers, then straight through a mass of gawkers. More and more these days, civilians stood in the open, taking pictures and video as they risked the one thing they and their parents held dearest in all the world – their lives. Dahl didn't understand: a few moments of adulation on social media couldn't be worth the risk.

An alleyway beckoned, dark and seemingly empty. Dahl risked a last glance back before herding the others into it.

Elements of the crowd were already returning to the Gardens, some people booing as they thought the Prime Minister had fled. No doubt, the PM's opposition was already finessing the idea that Sealy himself had planned the aborted assassination. Most would be hoping for information, showing their bravery and trying to snag a passing cop. Even more would be trying to jump before a camera and put their face on prime time. The stage and podium were deserted, now, but as he watched, Dahl thought he saw some of the mercs wandering around the edge of the stage. He couldn't be sure, just a brief sighting of black vests that didn't prove anything. But it was time to review all that Johanna and he had heard. It was time to get to the bottom of whatever the hell was going on tonight.

Fact: the business with Sealy was far more important to Grant and Vega than recapturing Dahl and his family. This was saying something – both men had every reason to see Dahl suffer and die.

Fact: Sealy was part of the setup, as was a bulky, rotten core of cops.

Fact: Johanna had overheard a conversation during her incarceration, but it had nothing to do with the PM's assassination.

Fact: Grant organized notoriously high-level incidents. Dahl could think of no other way to describe the man's stock in trade. He wove a black thread of chaos through the entire infrastructure of every place he operated in. While remaining inconspicuous, he created havoc and then moved on, the parasite of parasites, invisible in society both high and low.

Fact: Dahl and his family were situated in the middle of it all. A dangerous place to be, yes, but also an opportunity. Being in the middle meant they could affect the outcome. And after all this, and whatever Vega and Grant had planned, Dahl wanted very much to affect the outcome.

A small crowd coalesced in the Gardens, pulling together for a rousing cheer. Nothing happened up on stage. Sealy wasn't coming back. Some stayed put and called out: "Coward!" while others gave up and headed back to the parade. Dahl took his family deeper into the alleyway and gathered them around.

"Do you have any money, Dario?"

The lad fixed his chiseled jaw. "Not a dime."

"'cause that'd be too easy," Dahl muttered. *Or not.* Could he really rent a hotel room and leave Johanna and the kids behind? Not on this day, in this town right now. "Well, we can't stay here . . . " He wondered if the beach with all its layered darknesses would be safer; simply find the shelter of a stand of palm trees and lie low to await reinforcements. It seemed like as good a refuge as any.

"C'mon." He led them in that direction, striding down the alley, toward the seemingly endless parade.

"Are we going home, Daddy?" Isabella asked.

Julia was the first to answer her. "Don't worry, Iz. Dad will keep us safe."

"I really hate this vacation."

Julia hugged her sister close. "Me too. I want to go home."

Dahl walked ahead, close to Johanna. "It'll take time," he whispered, "but I think they'll be okay."

Johanna nodded. "I'm sure of it."

"You were an amazing mother today."

It sounded a little corny, even to his ears, but he could honestly say it came from the heart.

"Oh, Torsten, don't start me blubbering again. I need to get past all that."

He smiled, wondering how traumatic events made people see themselves in a stronger light and whether those new traits stayed with them. He prayed they'd live to find out.

"We have an awful lot of talking to do."

Johanna laughed hard, right there in the darkest alley in Barbados with the parade music pounding ahead and the stars glimmering above. With the children close to their sides. She laughed so hard she made herself burst out into fits of coughing. Dahl draped an arm around her shoulders and held tight; the closest they'd been for many months, in every way. He could feel Isabella's mooning eyes upon them and hear Julia's suppressed giggle. Thank god for little girls and their unquenchable, limitless spirit. Right now, there was no darkness around them except for a shadow cast by Dario's own recent loss, and Dahl meant to redress that barbarity before the sun rose.

They reached the far end of the alley a few moments later. Floats passed by, lit by myriad colors, outstanding in the night. The marchers were ten deep still, meandering around the barriers, snaking toward Independence Square. Side streets branched off in the general direction of the beach, giving Dahl the option he'd been hoping for.

"This way, stay close."

He merged with the crowd, only to hear shouts and sounds of pursuit coming from behind. The mercs he'd seen near the PM's emptied dais. Now pounding down the alley they'd just vacated.

Dahl cursed himself. He'd been so preoccupied with Sealy and the shock of discovering his betrayals that he'd ignored his training once more:

He'd failed to check Dario for tracking devices.

Never again.

Back to being the soldier. Time get to work.

But first they had to run.

THIRTY TWO

Dahl switched like a TV channel, instantly shedding the skin of a father and throwing on the soldier's armor. Beckoning Isabella and Julia, he urged them in front, straight into the parade and joined its flow. Johanna moved closely beside and Dario brought up the rear. The current took them. Dahl found himself alongside a six-foot-seven woman wearing a yellow peacock feather headdress and little else, another woman wearing a kitschy gown and a man twirling a cane, dressed as sharp as ZZ Top under his stunning, white suit. Ahead a whole line of marchers strutted and swaggered, twirled and stalked, the colors blinding, the noise overwhelming. It occurred to him that, remarkably, the incident with Sealy hadn't come close to shutting down the festivities or sent people fleeing. But taking in the sheer size and scope of the parade, he imagined that it would take something much more perilous. Besides, it seemed in the PM's best interest to leave everything running as normal. He too had chosen this day for a reason.

Dahl spun in place, checking for pursuit.

It still came. Heads bobbed as the group of mercs followed, running hard. Dahl saw three, maybe four. Grant, it seemed, hadn't given up on the Dahl family just yet and had added more locals to the chase. The rewards Vega could offer would make it an easy sell. Owning the country's Prime Minister no doubt had its benefits. Dahl dropped his shoulders and pushed the children to make them go faster. Together, they saw a gap and wedged through the line ahead, coming up to the rear of a high, wide float.

"Don't stop," Johanna breathed at his side. "They're still coming."

Good. Now he had two sets of eyes. Earlier today he'd barely been able to trust his own.

The float was purely makeshift, in true Bajan fashion. Made fast and easy, it was a thin metal frame, draped with many-hued fabrics, tied to the back of a pickup. The vehicle was festooned in colorful cloth as well, the driver barely able to see at his three-mile-per-hour crawl. In the bed of the vehicle, half a dozen festive bodies clapped and danced, holding banners and scarves and, apparently, anything they could lay their hands on.

Dahl ducked around the blind side, walking alongside the float, staying low. The kids moved well, carefully, remarkably undistracted by the float and the people and the noise. Sometimes it paid to stay covert and move steadier and he saw no reason not to try that approach right now. The riot of humanity here would work nicely in their favor. He raised an eye at Dario to remain on alert, indicating the side of the street. To their right, the barriers segregated the crowd from the marchers, and every so often they passed a vigilant policeman. Dahl hadn't seen one yet but had begun to formulate an explanation for when he did.

The route had reached a central part of the city, buildings towering over all but barely seen, even their light pinks and blues relegated to the shade by the mobile extravagance passing through. A rich aroma of blended fragrances rode the air, from barbecue smells to the zing of spicy seasoning and perfumed whiffs from hundreds of bodies dancing around. Cheers followed them every step of the way. Dahl kept eyes to front and rear, now confident that Johanna and Dario would do the same.

So far so good.

He indicated that Johanna should lead the kids and slipped back to Dario, knowing that their freedom would be short-lived unless he could relieve the lad of an item or two.

"We're being tracked," he shouted above the racket. "You have devices on you."

Dario screwed his face in confusion. "I do?"

"It must be you." Dahl knew Johanna had been wearing a bikini during her capture and nobody would have been able to secure anything to her person without her knowledge. He, too, had been similarly attired. Dario wore a gold watch, a narrow bracelet and a filigreed necklace. Chances were, his father had had him bugged.

"Sorry." Dahl removed the watch and threw it deep into the crowd. He followed suit with Dario's remaining jewelry and then eyed him calculatingly.

"Anything else?"

"No wallet." Dario said. "No keys. So unless it's sewn into the lining of my jeans . . ."

Dahl shrugged. "Anything's possible. But we'll not strip you just yet. Although—" he looked around. "You'd fit in quite well."

"Are you serious?"

Dahl had more crucial things to consider than Dario's embarrassment. "Do it," he said. "We'll grab you some more."

Dario tucked a hand into the waistband of his jeans just as Dahl saw the familiar bobbing heads.

One peered around the rear end of the float and smiled broadly. "They're here!" he called to his team.

"Move!" Dahl called to Johanna, and she needed no further warning. She immediately urged the children forward toward the pickup's front end. Dario spun, gun close to his now-naked thigh, but Dahl stopped him.

"Not here. Go with them."

Dahl ran hard at the man following them, regretting the choice he'd made. A gunshot here might start a stampede, killing many, but it remained a solid choice to stop the pursuit. Keep them safe.

Shocked at Dahl's move toward him, the man stopped and started to raise his gun. Too late. Dahl swiped him into the side of the float, following with an elbow to his head. The float ambled on beside them, and the crowd whooped it up as dancers grinned, singing in time and tune. Dahl took a blow to the side of the head. To his right, Johanna urged the girls ahead of the slow-moving truck, but Dario tarried, eyes on the fight.

"Go!" Dahl shouted. "Watch them."

His opponent landed a blow to the neck. Dahl fought fast and hard, with the desperation of a father losing his children. He had the edge on his opponent because of his military training, but no opponent could simply be left unconscious now.

He struck at the weak spots, the nerve clusters and tender areas, but Vega's merc proved tougher than he'd looked. His opponent had a fair amount of training. Dahl was aware that the bloodied man's friends couldn't be too far behind, whereas Dahl's family ranged farther away with each passing second. He backed away and kicked, landing a boot dead-square upon the man's chest, sending him crashing against the float trailer's metal edge. The bunting fluttered all around the man as his arms gyrated, even some thin wire getting twisted around his wrist. Now aware of him, the dancers began beating down upon him too, even as his skull bled and his legs wobbled. Dahl darted away, seeking his family.

Around the front of the float, more parade lines frolicked along the city street. Dahl saw Johanna flitting through the center of them. To his left, away towards the other curb, three tails pushed among the revelers. Dahl moved to intercept.

Another float trundled ahead, this one higher, richer in color, and more imposing. A yellow-garbed, dark-skinned woman rode the dizzy heights, waving to one and all, while below her several men and women danced around the float's perimeter, each sporting feathers and beads over their outlandish costumes.

The three men saw Dahl before he reached them, and one angled to cut him off. A second man cast around for his lost colleague before making a beeline for Dahl. The other continued after Johanna. Dahl changed course, bending his brisk, forceful walk in that direction too, figuring it would be better to be beside his family than apart.

Circumstance and fate pushed them together, and then apart.

The float came between them, the celebrators bunched all around. Dahl lost his prey and the men lost him. For a moment. Dahl worked his way past the float, looking all around the garish scene for Johanna. For a moment, he saw only a sea of bobbing heads, darkness outside the streetlights, and carnival everywhere, but then Johanna's blonde hair stood out like a bare bulb in a cave and gave him a focal point. He moved insistently in that direction, ignoring the protests. As he reached them, a pair of police officers took an interest.

"You shouldn't be in there," one shouted from where he leaned against a barrier. "Come on out. Parade only."

His partner looked bored. Dahl pushed past and tried to merge with the crowd, finally reaching Dario, but the cop continued to shout.

"Get out of there!"

Marking them.

Dahl saw the cop's car up ahead, parked at an angle across a side-road to ensure the parade didn't go astray. This particular cop had gotten a bee in his bonnet, and Dahl didn't think it was malicious, but it was drawing unwanted attention their way. He'd gotten a little turned around but thought the next side street that angled off

162

should lead toward the beach. Trouble was, they couldn't let their pursuers know their intentions. And time was wasting away. Dahl knew waiting for the cavalry was in itself a good strategy, but he didn't want Vega to make his own terrible plans and then disappear; he didn't want Sealy to get through all this unchallenged; and he especially didn't want Nick Grant to vanish into the wilderness, only to reappear at a later date.

Dahl regretted it even before he executed it, but quashed the guilt and put his family first. A cloth animal bounded ahead of him, fabric draped over two men to make them look vaguely like a giant bat, complete with makeshift wings. Dahl pushed alongside and steered them toward the cop car, grabbing hold of the framework beneath the material and using brute strength to amend their course. The men, part of the structure, moved easily, quite possibly as unsighted as everyone else seemed to be. They collided with the front of the vehicle, giving both cops something more important to worry about. Dahl surveyed the dipping bodies all around, saw his three pursuers – now united again – through the throng.

"Keep moving," he told Dario. "I'll try to draw them away."

"Don't lose us." Johanna shouted, pointing at a sign up ahead.

To the Beach.

Dahl nodded. *Great minds* . . . He wouldn't lead the locals that way and might not find his family for the very best of reasons – if they found good shelter, they wouldn't want it compromised. The dancers flowed around a wide, easy corner, another tall float appearing ahead. Dahl sensed rather than saw their attackers closing and leaped instinctively for his kids. A fist connected with his temple, smashing his head sideways, neck creaking. Spots danced before his eyes but he shrugged the pain away. He caught the man's next punch with an open palm, then closed his fist over his opponent's knuckles, crushing hard. The other two figures approached his family, only a few strides away from Johanna now. Dahl could no longer keep this low-key. The three men would end here.

He plowed into his opponent, caught a good bunch of shirt and jacket in each hand, bent his knees and heaved. Feet kicked as they left the asphalt. Eyes blinked rapidly in disbelief. A low vocal note signified horror as the owner became a 200-pound bowling ball, hurled at his friends. The trio went down hard, leaving them open to rapid assault.

Dahl smashed one across the face but got tangled with the third. As he fell to his knees, he saw the fourth man now returned, coming at Johanna from behind.

"Look—" A fist stopped his warning cold, drawing blood, rattling teeth.

Johanna turned, saw the man who threatened her and the girls and threw a swift punch that connected directly with the already-injured man's nose, stopping him dead. Dahl was so shocked he took another punch from the rising second man of the trio. He swiveled and delivered a martial-arts combination to throat, eyes and ears that rendered his opponent comatose. The bowling ball was still struggling, now being kicked and pushed around by marchers. Dahl finished him with a rabbit punch to the back of the neck.

Now the third man was rising to his feet. Dahl kicked him point-blank in the temple, and screams erupted all around as the man dropped, unconscious or worse. It might be seen as a spirited skirmish, or it might be seen for what it was. Dahl couldn't concern himself with style.

Only one opponent now remained standing, glaring at Johanna, bloody-nosed, with something like wounded wonder.

"*Back. Off.*" She stood in front of her children, the primordial protector.

The man didn't comply so Johanna struck again. This time he deflected the blow, but by then Dahl was alongside. He targeted where he knew the guy was already weak – where the truck earlier made contact with his skull – made devastating contact and gathered his family.

"Quickly now."

They angled in the direction of the next side road, again cutting through the lines of marchers to angry protests. Ahead, a mammoth, vividly-decked float attracted most of the attention, in particular the half-naked dancing men and women on top. Dahl apologized as he barged people aside, pulling Isabella and Julia along behind. Refuge for his family, if not complete freedom, waited just a few dozen strides away.

And then a shot rang out.

THIRTY THREE

It was the stuff of nightmares; the unmistakable sound of a rifle shot resounding across the parade, with Dahl knowing it was wholly his problem and at any moment the next bullet might take his children, or his wife. He thought he saw the first bullet glance off the road ahead, carve out a ragged furrow, and then ricochet into the night. Although he couldn't tell for sure, it seemed as though the shot had come from above.

Sniper.

The tables had turned. Earlier he had thought a sniper might be about to take the Prime Minister out – now it was entirely possible the PM had arranged this hit.

"Duck and run!" he shouted, voice betraying his fear. "Just go. *Go!*"

They sprinted like Olympic runners freed from a mantrap and chased by cheetahs. They broke through the remaining marchers and left the newly forming chaos behind. Dahl tried to see their assailant as he ran, tried to look around and up. The attempt was beyond useless; it slowed him and almost tripped him up. Johanna shouted at him to focus ahead and, again, he was stunned. Essentially, safety was his job – but his family was in too much peril to strip emotion away, even though that was the requirement.

Not today.

Behind, the music continued and many of the party animals, both real and pretend, paraded on. Some broke ranks, looking for cops; others backed away with terrified glances to the rooftops. Seconds passed, long seconds, turning into double figures.

"Head to the beach," Dahl said. "Quickly now."

Dahl felt immensely inept when the second shot rang out, unable to process until it happened and then was gone, the bullet traveling at thousands of miles per hour, taking Dario up high and spinning him around. The lad's gun threatened to fall out of his waistband and skid away, not that he'd shown any penchant to use it, but snagged its sights on a belt-hoop and stayed in place. A spray of red misted the air. Dario collapsed face first, hitting the ground with a cry of agony. Dahl didn't break stride for a moment, bending as he ran and hoping to every God of strength and agility and power that he had the potency to succeed. Even as Johanna screamed, he bent low and scooped up the still-falling figure, taking him around the waist and heaving with every muscle, every sinew, every stretched tendon. Dario came up off the beachside walkway with a heave but immediately unbalanced Dahl as his head sagged low. Dahl shuffled the bulk along, trying to regain stability. The entrance to the side-street that led to the beach beckoned ahead. Unrest escalated among the paraders left behind. Dahl pushed hard beyond his limits, unable to prevent a roar escaping his mouth.

Had Dario become the main target?

What did that mean?

Vega's hit, perhaps? Grant's?

It didn't escape his attention that whoever was firing would be able to see their route, at least some part of it.

They arrived at the sand at a rapid pace, Johanna herding the girls along and Dahl carrying Dario. The Swede had no issues in dealing with the bullet wound. It had entered the lad's shoulder, but was nothing more than a flesh wound. He'd handled many before, most in the field, but knew they had to reach safety first. You could dress a wound under fire, yes, but not viably with a wife and kids in danger alongside.

Dahl shifted Dario as they ran, not losing a jot of pace, simply seeking to make the young man more comfortable. Johanna looked over, eyes as round as saucers. Dahl nodded.

"He'll be okay."

The beach was quiet, the small structures of refreshment huts and watersport stands either dimly illuminated or cast into pitch blackness. Dahl thought he could see the silent, black swell of the ocean ahead and the soft glow of an errant lamp, painting a subtle swathe across the beach. They didn't let up until the ocean landscape grew large, the sand almost at their toes. Then Dahl cast around fast, sending questing glances back the way they'd come.

No signs of pursuit.

"What do you think that was?" Johanna asked.

"Not a clue."

"How is he?"

"We'll find out."

Dahl pounded across the sand now, unable to give his family the reassurances they needed, trusting they would follow closely. The edges of the beach were bordered by high fences and overhanging trees, thick with dense shadow. He aimed toward the darkest, most viscous area and knelt, letting Dario slide gently to the sand.

"I . . . I'm okay . . ." the kid gasped, a good sign.

Dahl fought away frustration. Not only was he running blind with his family without money, knowledge and ID, but he was now also being called upon to patch a bullet wound on the beach with no equipment. He checked the wound in Dario's shoulder first, probed the ragged hole while clamping a hand over Dario's mouth. Johanna removed the children by several feet. Dahl turned Dario slightly, saw the exit hole in the top of the muscle.

"Got lucky," he said. "Went right through. No bones

168

broken." He smiled. "My usual team would say it doesn't really count as being shot. Just a scratch."

"Feels . . . like fire and ice and . . . knives."

"Stop whining." Dahl ripped a strip from Johanna's shawl, cleaned the wound as best he could with the larger part and then used the clean strip to bandage the wound. He wrapped it tight. It would do for now, and Dario would need painkillers and antibiotics, but Dahl found it highly unlikely they'd find a pharmacy at the beach. Saying that, the number of times he'd already been asked if he wanted to buy Charlie, even with the kids along, was astounding. He'd known from before that "Charlie" was a Barbados staple and on most locals' lips. Nobody had to score drugs in Barbados to know what the resident painkiller was called. It would take Dario's pain away for a short while, but it would also dull every other sense he possessed.

Dahl needed him whip-sensitive, hyper-alert, ultra-vigilant.

He leaned over the boy. "You all right?"

"I don't know. Never been shot before."

"I have. And you won't get any sympathy from me. Now, can you help keep my family alive? At least your belt buckle saved your bloody gun."

"Yes. Hand me that gun and I'll fight an army."

"Good. Very good." Dahl sat back and beckoned the others closer. "Because we need to think. And plan. And end this."

THIRTY FOUR

Dahl took a breather but didn't waste more than two minutes. A sense of incredulity fell over the others, and Dahl saw it as something along the lines of battle trauma – never good and especially when they remained in harm's way. The silence helped, though.

Helped him think.

What next?

Darkness was their ally, pooling all around and permeating a beautiful silence. The one time they heard noises he picked it up 100 feet away, saw the figures and knew it was a pair of alcohol-toting romancers before they'd gotten ten feet. They found their own darkness, far enough away, unaware of the Dahls, and got straight down to business.

Ironically, this new safety had returned them to where they started this afternoon – the beach. That brought him around to Grant, then Vega and finally Prime Minister Sealy. A semblance of justice had to be meted out. More than that. The first two in particular were men who used the world as a deadly playground, stomping over civilians and governments wherever they chose to go, dealing misery without care or concern. Vega may have his so-called 'family' loyalties, but Grant certainly did not.

And both had a score to settle with Dahl.

As it seemed now, so did Sealy. Dahl accepted that Dario was now with them, and that meant protecting the kid with almost the same fervor he'd protect his own flesh and blood.

He saw Johanna watching him. "They have to be stopped."

"I'm not sure how we can do that."

He felt a swell of emotion inside. The sudden use of *we;* the neutral question rather than the immediate *negative.* "You're a constant surprise, love."

She beckoned the girls closer, now that Dario seemed stable. "Isn't that what marriage is supposed to be?"

Dahl hesitated. Interesting use of words, encompassing past and future possibilities and even an opening for Dahl, but they had to stay on point.

"Grant. Vega. Sealy. They're together for a reason, something huge. They wouldn't need the Facilitator here if it wasn't big."

"Well, remembering the conversation I overheard," Johanna said. "And taking it in different context, you're right: they are here together. Some kind of meeting."

"We have to stop them finishing up and leaving," Dahl said again.

"I won't leave my children. Not for anything."

Dahl had already felt a certain weight winched up and away from him. This happened when they found a relative safe haven. Now, another burden fell away. He was convinced he could rely upon Johanna and Dario to keep Isabella and Julia safe no matter the cost, even if it meant losing their own lives.

Dahl said: "I have to go. I can't let . . . this happen around me."

"I know."

"This meeting – or whatever it is – could be over well before our help arrives. I've seen deals made in a tent, over in fifteen minutes, that changed the course of the world. I've seen handshakes in the street that greenlit terrorist strikes. If those three men are here, now, the outcome of whatever they're discussing could be devastating."

"I understand," Johanna said. "This man, Grant, is the worst of his kind. The things he said . . . about . . ." She swallowed drily as she glanced toward the children. "I'd never repeat."

"I know."

"The world would be better without him."

Dahl smiled grimly. "Will be," he said. "Will be."

"He holds a grudge against you."

"For a long time now." Dahl nodded. "He holds me responsible for the death of his wife and daughter. The worst part of it is – I see his point of view. I see through his eyes, *his* mentality, and know how he arrived at that point. But it's garbage. Twisted, perverse logic that, deep down, he knows contradicts every fact of the event. He knows, but yearns for some kind of revenge."

"Be careful, Torsten."

She didn't pile on the questions. No guilt. No second-guessing. Just an acceptance that he had to end this now, tonight, or they'd be suffering through the rest of their lives and through the generations.

Dahl placed a hand on her arm. "I will. You know me."

"The Mad Swede? I don't think so."

Dahl saw a sadder future, where he abandoned his family and sought out their enemies, only to return and find he'd truly lost everything. Maybe Johanna and Dario couldn't protect the kids. *He* was the soldier after all.

You can't just leave Vega and Grant out there, wandering the world like viruses.

More to the point, what would stop Vega or Grant seeking them out next week, or next year?

"If I don't return, you know what to do."

Johanna squeezed his hand. "I hate to hear you say that but, yes, I know who to talk to."

"They'll bring thunder and lightning. They'll make Grant's world a volcanic wasteland."

"So I've heard."

"You'll be safe if you trust them."

"I want *you*, Torsten. Not them. I really do."

Dahl struggled to remain focused. Isabella and Julia peered around their mother's side, eyes deep and wet and impossible to discount. The love that radiated from his children's eyes melted his heart.

And hardened his will. He had to end the larger threat.

For you. For your future and your mother's future and to slow the destruction of a thousand other futures.

He studied Dario and checked the makeshift bandage he'd fashioned from Jo's shawl. The outflow of blood had reduced to a trickle. The quandary remained. Good sense dictated that he return to one of the many refreshment stands and appropriate juices and food, in particular for Dario, but harsh reality told him every second he didn't pursue Grant was one more nail hammered deep in someone's coffin.

He reviewed his options once more: He could keep on running with his family, leave them and seek help, or stay and protect them. Each of those options meant worrying about creeping consequences later.

Or he could proceed as planned.

For my family and for others, I will stand my ground.

THIRTY FIVE

Dahl borrowed Dario's gun, still with six bullets in the mag, two guns now giving him double the firepower, and turned his thoughts toward a new dilemma. Where would Grant even be? How did you locate a trio of cockroaches in the entirety of Barbados? Before he could apply his mind to that, he still had to say a few painful goodbyes. There was no way of rationalizing what he was about to do. The Mad Swede had stayed quiet until now; the dark side had to have its day. To explain, to justify one action in the face of all the others he could carry out, was beyond him; but it was clear *within* him. Inside every layer, every pore, every pulsing blood vessel.

"Good luck," Johanna said. "I love you. Now, go."

And there it was, laid out better than he could have put it, so clean and pure it was like a fresh snowfall.

Two young people didn't quite see it that way, hanging onto his arms because of the doubts they had. Everything they had been through today had not only depleted all their reserves and overwhelmed their minds, it had also helped them recognize at least one vital ideal Dahl had been trying to teach them all their young lives.

Family. If you were lucky enough to have a loving, caring family, you should fight to hold on to it, fight and scrap and brawl for it until your nails were bloody, your voice ragged, your options spent. *Fight.*

They clung to him and he knelt to face them.

"Only *we* can look after each other, Dad," Isabella said in her light sing-song voice. "That's what you say." Her eyes were earnest, deep as pools.

"We can only fully rely on each other," he said. "Just family. Just us. That's what I meant."

"Then why are you leaving?" Julia asked.

He coughed to give himself a moment. "To make us safe forever."

His children accepted it but still clung on, probably relying on what instinct told them at a profound level. Johanna felt to her knees beside them and said more soothing words.

"Let Dad go to work," she said finally.

"Be back soon to tuck you in," he said and turned to Johanna. Quickly, he laid out his plan both for her and for Dario.

Then he walked away.

The streets of Bridgetown still reeled from the festive assault, the main arteries clogged to near impassable. Oblivious revelers crowded together, many weary from the night's fun but just as many using the carnival as a mere warm-up act to the main event. Sirens split the night air, common in any major city, and the presence of cops and marshals only served to instil a broodier, perturbed air in the crowd. Ambulances crept slowly through the throng, and any casualties would be put down to the density of people and intensities of the celebrations – at least for now. Dahl still had the city map Johanna had snagged earlier but the main focus of his thoughts rested around where he believed his quarry would be.

Grant. Vega. Sealy. Working together. Meeting together after the parade, or after the speech. That made more sense, and meant Sealy would have to follow some kind of protocol. If he'd been meeting local trendsetters say, or a celeb or even a visiting dignitary, the PM might have whisked them away to a high-profile restaurant or luxurious hotel. But criminals? Even faceless ones?

As a head of state, he would take them to the same place he'd take any politician, banker or Wall Street investor.

He'd take them to his residence.

Dahl's theory derived partly from logic, but mostly from experience – where else would these figureheads of misconduct feel safe enough to discuss their plans? Nowhere else in Barbados fit that particular bill.

Dahl took a moment to conceal the handgun as best he could and tidy himself up in the reflection of a shop window. Considering all that had happened today, he didn't feel too bad physically. Bruises and scrapes would heal, and were necessary, truth be told. No way did he want to come out of this day looking as if nothing had happened. The backup he'd called would show no remorse with their biting wit . . .

Once they knew everyone was safe.

Dahl checked the map, which pinpointed the PM's residence as near the St. Lawrence Gap. He traced his finger along Government Hill, past Two Mile Hill, and then came to Illaro Court, Sealy's home for what the PM imagined would be a little while longer.

A good 30-minute walk. Maybe more.

He set out, wondering if he might be able to thumb a ride, then remembering he couldn't trust anyone, even cops. He now took out the phone he'd stolen earlier, checked his team status, and advised them where to find his family. It was risk-free – he couldn't imagine Sealy having a listening station – and one way of setting his mind at rest. Preparing for the hour or so ahead.

They were still a few hours out. Truth be told he'd been hoping for better news, maybe even a little help, but here he was. Trusting no one.

Except your family.

Isabella and Julia's faces swam around his conscience

and Dahl made himself stop, breathe deeply, and tried to remember the soldier he'd been only a few days ago. One thing was certain – he'd never survive without the soldier within.

Only ending this tonight would end it forever, he reminded himself.

But Torsten Dahl, normally the man who brought the full force, felt like half an army.

THIRTY SIX

Illaro Court was a walled residence, set back not far off a main road. Dahl studied its picturesque surroundings as he walked, picking out several thick stands of trees that might prove useful, all dotted around half-a-dozen well-kept lawns. The main wrought-iron gates were closed, the white pillars to either side not terribly imposing but mounted with CCTV units. Of course, Dahl had no intention of using the front gate. A long walk around the residence revealed St. Barnabas Heights, a small housing development backing onto Illaro Court. Dahl found no difficulties in reaching the trees that bounded the PM's property walls. The issue now was cameras. This far away he hoped there would be none; it seemed a little overkill, but as he approached the wall itself, Dahl knew his odds lessened with every step.

Darkness pressed at his every pore, smothering his face with a welcome anonymity. The ground beneath his feet was soft, squelchy, as if it had been watered recently. Twigs littered the pathways, forcing him to tread lightly. A faint scent wafted through the night, smoked meat perhaps, reminding him that he couldn't remember the last time he'd eaten properly. He'd already skirted most of the high wall and found it solid up to this point, and not overlooked. The point where he gazed now, however, saw it bend away from the houses, through an area of open ground and past one solitary tree. The good news was that it also bordered the extreme rear of the mansion's lawn.

He cinched what was left of the shawl tighter around his waist, ensuring the guns stayed put, then climbed the lone tree, taking great care.

The truth was he saw no sign of cameras. Most likely, they were positioned around the inside exterior of the property, along with all the other security devices he came across quite frequently in his line of work. His state of mind declared quite openly that he was entering this residence one way or the other, so to hell with any cameras he couldn't actually see.

Once he was able to see over the wall, Dahl paused. A wide, rectangular parking area led to the house, which was an old, two-story affair with balconies and railings, extensions and too many windows to count. The parking area revealed the haphazard arrangement of the PM's limo and two black Range Rovers. If he were a betting man, Dahl would put his lunch on the vehicles being the very ones that abducted Johanna.

There appeared to be a smaller building beside the parking area, maybe a storage shed or guardhouse. Dahl saw three men outside, none of them vigilant, two standing together talking and the other leaning against the limo, smoking a cigarette. A careful study of the residence, its sides and bordering trees, revealed no other signs of life. Cameras on poles stood well-spaced out, and there were probably more fixed to the eaves of the house. If so, Dahl couldn't spy them in the dark.

Nevertheless, he moved forward, never back. In sync with his day's luck so far the tree branches were all much too flimsy to carry him over the wall, so he put his back against the moss-covered stone, his feet on the solid tree trunk, and used a method he called 'chimneying' to ascend. Foot to hand, slide up with the back, other foot to hand, and so on, an inch at a time until he neared the top of the wall. Still hidden, he paused, wishing the fire he'd started along the length of his spine would peter out. Now came the hardest part. Flexing his thighs he twisted around so that he could peer over the top of the wall, then waited until fortune cast a welcome shadow over the proceedings. The shadow eventually came as Dahl's twisted muscles moved along the pain gauge from merely agonizing to absolute torture, and as the three men appeared to end their conversations and retire to the guardhouse. Perhaps this had been their hourly patrol; Dahl wasn't sure, but he used the few minutes' grace to manipulate his frame onto the top of the wall and then to slip over.

Landing feet first, he crouched low, absorbing the impact and making less noise than a falling branch. Stars glittered far above, but shadows still ruled the night, draping their all-encompassing shrouds from his head to his toes. Stark light pooled nearer the house. No security lights flashed on and off, because the guards would ask for them to be disabled, and he saw no nestling cameras anywhere around the eaves.

Can't be this easy.

Dahl's experience told him that you couldn't deal with things you couldn't see. Who knew how carefully guarded this residence was? He wasn't talking about the White House here, but infra-red and lasers, pressure pads and sensors were all possibilities. Dahl decide to deal with that problem if and when it arose. There were options — both for escape and attack — and he'd committed them to memory now. Sealy and his entourage were already hunting him – what did he have to lose?

Knowledge and skill also told him to take his time; his own know-how would win through and reveal an answer. His steps were short, his movements contained. He remained attuned to every rustle and crunch, made himself grow accustomed to the dull, distant laughs and cheers coming from the guardhouse so that the moment they changed timbre he would know. He examined every inch of the way ahead before each precise step, just in case more guards were out there.

His precautions paid off.

Positioned in shadow, far ahead between the wall and the house, he saw a dark figure make a transferal of weight, heard the faint rattle of a weapon against rough bark. A man stood there, a silent watcher.

There would be others.

No mind. Dahl was a Special Forces ghost, stealing the light as he glided along, embracing the dark with intimate ease. Some of Sealy's men might be military trained, but not a man among them would have Dahl's experience, his expertise. This was business as usual; a deliverance from evil dressed in a t-shirt, swim-shorts and wearing a shawl.

Dahl skirted the man, taking long minutes to make just a few steps, noticing a bare window beyond him where he could at least get a peek inside the house. The maneuver completed, he raised his head at the side of the window, quickly glimpsing the interior. All he saw was a wood-paneled empty room, golden lights picking out brass fixings and light fittings. Hardcover books lined a ceiling-length bookcase, old-school reading for old-school men. Working his way along, he found two more bare windows before calculating he was now still some way from the edge of the house and unavoidable detection. He'd viewed only one person inside the house thus far — a man wearing an expensive suit and carrying a glass of champagne. A stranger.

Dahl sank down to his haunches, back to the wall, and stared out over the lawn. He was as safe here as anywhere, unmoving and shadow-draped and pressed into a man-size gap offered by a jutting extension to the house.

Life had turned since he first met Nick Grant, both men revolving around different axes. For Dahl it had been about strict morality, hard work and loyalty. Grant's axis ran through the bones of others, drenched in blood, fixed with a hatred for Dahl so intense it was tangible. It occurred to Dahl now that he'd lived under the shadow of Grant's projected guilt for far too long.

The Facilitator, as was his wont, had made a deal with a faction of the Russian *mafiya*. Back then, Grant had a family – a wife and daughter – wholly unaware of who and what the man they poured every ounce of their trust into actually was.

"Did you return it?" Dahl whispered into the darkness, no louder than the flight of a passing mosquito. "As best you could?"

This had been years after the Amazon jungle episode. Dahl's team had become aware of the Russian gang and their crimes. No mention of Grant had been made. As their surveillance of the Russians became more complete, they learned the true depths to which the *mafiya* members were plummeting – human trafficking, body-part acquisitions, assassinations.

A man in a lofty office crunched some numbers and slid his order down the long chain – they had to act. Dahl's team prepped and went in and, for the most part, the operation went as expected.

One or two Russians escaped, their boss among them, and went into hiding.

"Never saw you," Dahl whispered again to the dark night in place of Nick Grant. "Never even knew you were part of it."

When the dust settled, everyone moved on. Months passed. It was only later that Dahl heard how the surviving Russians meted out their vengeance. Never renowned for having the best grasp of whole situations, they blamed everyone but themselves for the *lapse*, as they called it, the failure to safeguard their business. Heads rolled, literally. Dahl learned of the fallout, but the mysterious Man on High never ordered any further payback.

Probably didn't fit his business plans at the time.

The Facilitator's reputation had been, to that point, unblemished. Luckily, most of his clients trusted Russians about as much as they trusted their own mothers, but unluckily for Grant, the Russians were uncomplicated about whom they took out their anger on. Everyone got a taste. When Grant made himself scarce, they sent men to take vengeance on the Facilitator's wife and daughter.

"I'm sorry," Dahl whispered into the Barbadian night. "Not for you, Grant, but for the innocent."

Grant blamed Dahl – the initial takedown team's leader – for the Russians' vengeance and let it be known, globally, that one day, one way or another, he would claim back all he had lost. Dahl had made quiet investigations, trying to learn the reason for this new threat against him. In doing so, he'd discovered Nick Grant's role in the *mafiya* operation that his task force and he had dismantled. And learned how the Russians had spent weeks tracking Grant, losing him, and then turning their attention to his family, so that they could carry out their abominable version of justice. Not that they themselves lasted long. A couple of years later they vanished from all knowledge, evidently victims of Grant's own wrath. But in their decision of allowing Grant to live they had unknowingly wreaked a kind of vengeance upon Dahl, giving birth to Grant's undying vendetta.

Allowing Grant to live turned out to be the surviving Russians' real revenge on Dahl.

The Facilitator grew and grew after that, a warped solar flare, bringing incalculable sins to every place he touched. Each success fed the greed, inviting in worse nightmares that crawled and slithered and crept as they begged to be unleashed. Grant became a legend, and Dahl let it pass.

He checked his surroundings again. Still no sounds or movement nearby.

Enough thinking. He couldn't delay the inevitable.

He had to get inside.

He turned to the nearest window, tested it. Of course, it wouldn't budge, not even a millimeter. On the plus side, no sudden scraping noises gave away his position. He tried each window in turn, but to no avail.

No way in.

For normal people, anyway.

Dahl spun as footsteps crunched along the ground behind him.

THIRTY SEVEN

The shadow within shadows was a man, broad and chewing gum as he walked almost point-blank into the motionless Dahl. Though he had the advantage of surprise, Dahl was so shocked himself that he didn't put as much as he should have into the first punch. Consequently, the guard only went down to his knees, eyes glazed and weapon dropping from one limp hand. He batted up at Dahl weakly, then opened his mouth to sound an alarm, but the Mad Swede already had it covered. He landed a foot in the center of the man's face, kicking hard, and followed up without losing ground. His knee came down hard on his opponent's sternum, his large hand clamping the bloodstained mouth.

Relieved to see he'd lost nothing after today's rigors, he made sure the guard was out before dragging him into deeper darkness. Now the clock was well and truly ticking. He wouldn't kill this man, a fellow soldier and likely an innocent security staffer, which meant he now had a finite amount of time until the guard awoke. He checked the guard for communications devices and found that he was hooked up to a Bluetooth transmitter. Dahl took the man's weapon and broke the Bluetooth device, hoping that if it were tested in any way, it would initially be seen as a glitch and buy Dahl a little more time.

Holding the guard's weapon – a reliable, simple and accurate 9mm Glock 19, the bodyguard's perfect weapon, with a blued finish – down along his thigh, Dahl applied logic to the problem at hand. Of course the guard would have access to the house itself –but in what form? He patted the man down, finding a simple oblong of plastic like a credit card in the unconscious man's back pocket.

This would be a slide-reader then, allowing access much like a hotel key card . . . the question being exactly how much access?

A veteran, armed guard like the downed man should have almost total access, Dahl reasoned. He used the man's leather belt to secure him as fully as he was able.

Let's test that theory then.

First problem: which door? He couldn't just waltz in through the front, and even if he did manage to don the guard's clothing, he would look like an impostor. The odds were dire, but Dahl had to try.

No way did this house possess only one or two doors. Dahl inched his way around another sliver of property, slipping past another guard before finding a black alcove beneath a strip-window. The thick metal door had a card reader, which Dahl quickly utilized. Some men may have waited, worried, or backed off, but the Mad Swede's dogma had always been to keep moving forward. Reach the end and take the prize. Finish it.

With silent efficiency, the door cracked open. Dahl pushed slowly, still holding the gun low. The interior hall was narrow and dimly lit, probably adjusted to aid the guards' eyesight when they entered during the night. He slipped along the first hallway and then paused. A high-ceilinged reception room stood before him, trimmed exactly the same as the others he'd seen, dark and deep and polished. A two-flight staircase doubled back on itself to give access to the second floor. Dahl paused, seeing the yawning gap to the foot of the stairs as a deadly no-man's-land. He surveyed up and down and skimmed over every panel, seeing no sign of CCTV cameras. Yes, some versions were so small these days that he might not spot them but, as before, the soldier could only deal with what he knew. Dahl had seen them all, worked with them all, even watched as they were installed in his team's new offices. Gut instinct told him he was safe.

Footsteps rang out across the floor. Dahl slunk lower as a man passed by the opening and turned up the stairs. He wore waiter's attire and carried a silver platter upon which stood three full glasses of champagne.

Interesting.

But by no means conclusive. Sealy could entertain his guests in any one of the rooms of the house. Dahl allowed the waiter time to press ahead and then broke cover, slipping around the internal wall and into another offshoot. The way ahead was again little more than a pool of darkness, but Dahl scooted down the hallway and listened outside every closed door, just in case. The man he'd knocked unconscious wouldn't be stirring yet, but time remained short. Dahl finished with the first corridor and then hurried to try a second. The third led to the kitchen, if the muffled sounds of pans shifting and utensils clicking were anything to go by. Dahl ignored that door, though his stomach rebelled.

Another wing beckoned. It took him three minutes of intense skulking to rule it out. Not a soul stirred. On the way back, he had to pause when a clerk suddenly appeared ahead, seeking out a room and disappearing inside. Late for somebody to be working, he mused, but then governments never stopped. Silence drifted all around him and the old, polished walls watched broodily. Dahl stalked the halls, counting the minutes down in his head.

Cutting it bloody close.

Now for the staircase. Dahl waited in the shadow of a huge, ticking grandfather clock, growing accustomed to the house's noises again before making his move. A swift dart back and forth and he was on the top-floor landing, seeking refuge with swift, practiced eyes. An alcove gave momentary respite and a chance to reconnect with the house.

Footsteps approached.

Dahl didn't panic but flattened his back into the alcove and reached behind for a door knob. Finding it, he turned, readied the gun and pushed his way into the room. Expecting the worst, he found himself in a black space, the only light granted by undrawn drapes fastened back at an angle, allowing the stars to lend a silvery hue to the room. Dahl didn't have time to close the door, so left it open a crack and held his breath.

The footsteps stopped right outside.

He sensed that the door was being studied, proven right a moment later when it was pushed from the outside, swinging wide open. He fell to the floor instantly, as soundless as a dust mote, but inclined the barrel of the gun to a 45-degree angle.

All this, only to fail now.

But Dahl stayed professional, assuming nothing. The door struck the wall bumper softly, a slender figure outlined against the darker hall. Dahl crouched in silence, only a few feet away and to the woman's right. Hopefully she wouldn't look down. Hopefully she'd go about her duties. Dahl could tell by her uniform and the heap of bedding she held that she was a house cleaner. *Bad luck.* She'd probably just made up this room and remembered closing the door.

He could hear her gentle breathing and the soft swish of her clothing as she turned to survey the rest of the room. Her legs below the hem of her skirt were so close he could have blown on them, no doubt giving her the shock of her life. For one moment, he thought she might turn and walk away, no harm done, but then some deeper sense must have jarred her brain, as it often did with civilians, and made her look down.

Dahl rose alongside like a bad dream, anxious to clamp her mouth and stop the scream. One hand covered her lips, the other pressed firmly against the back of her head.

Frightened, flitting eyes stared over the top of his fingers; the rest of her stayed immobile. Carefully, he bent her head so she could see the gun he'd left on the floor. Her neck muscles fought against him but he took care not to manhandle her.

With a gentle foot, he eased the door shut, then whispered into her ear.

"I have no issue with you. I'm not here for you. Do you understand?"

A slight nod.

"Also, I don't trust you, love. Not one bit. Do you understand that?"

Another nod, this time with a stiffening of fear through her body.

"I won't hurt you unless you fight me. But I have to do this."

Dahl kept one hand over her mouth and pushed her further into the room with pressure at the small of her back. He made her pause and reached down to pick up the gun, noticing how still she went. This seemed to be the right time to tell her to remove her nylons – an order he'd not been looking forward to, since he wanted her to feel less threatened, not more. He kept his tone even and used the weapon as an obvious counterpoint. It worked. She bent slightly, raised her skirt and worked the hose down. Dahl looked up at the ceiling, making it obvious, trying not to break into an aimless whistle.

"Sorry," he said as she handed him the warm material. "Aren't you bloody hot in here?"

"I am local," she mumbled. "He sets the air too low."

"Ah."

Dahl held the nylons and cast around for the one other item he would need. Something from one of the drawers, probably. An interconnecting door stood to the left, offering further possibilities. Steering her over, he rummaged through the first set of drawers, found nothing except a few dog-eared books, and moved to the next. Here he found a man's vest and gave it a quick sniff.

"We're okay," he said. "It's clean."

Working against a nagging conscience, he tied the vest across her mouth to make a gag and then tied her wrists behind her back with the nylons. The woman's eyes flinched and jerked around as her fear rose, but Dahl consistently held out a palm and tried not to pinch or trap any skin. When he was finished, he turned her around to face him.

"I'll leave you here," he said. "But don't struggle. Plenty of guys I know would have cold-cocked you and left you bleeding into the carpet." He paused, unable to come up with anything else since it felt as if he were standing still and time was passing by in a V8 muscle car, with its mad, feral brother Destiny at the wheel. He showed the woman the other side of the bed and helped situate her so that she remained hidden from the door. It was all he could do. He wouldn't restrain her further, instead giving her a reason to stay quiet.

"I'll be waiting both inside and outside of this room," he said. "For the right time. No noise."

She nodded and he walked away, cracked the door and studied the hallway. Nothing moved, but the *tick-tock* of the grandfather clock downstairs echoed loudly through the shadowy halls. Dahl decided on a way to go and squeezed out of the room, following the solid wall to the next door and placing an ear close. Paintings hung along the walls on both sides, previous Prime Ministers probably, dozens of pairs of eyes watching him with various expressions of pride and guilt. All heads of state differed; some would fit into the corruptible camp and some wouldn't. All were tested.

Another door and another clamorous quiet. This house

was so calm a deaf man would hear a pin drop. That thought made Dahl move even more slowly and with care. It was at the end of this corridor, as a hallway branched off in both directions, that he heard the distant shuffle of feet. Not footsteps, but a shifting of weight.

He paused, listening. Eventually he decided the unknown stalemate was getting him nowhere, bent low, and slowly pushed his head forward so that he could peer around the corner at an odd angle, anomalous to the human perception in case someone was watching. Slowly, the scene unfolded – a long hallway that, by his current knowledge of the house, ran the length of two rooms, and a dogleg at the far end, running away from him. It was at this far end that a man stood, leaning against the wall and looking extremely bored, yawning even.

The rifle placed at his side, barrel against the wall, looked far less apathetic.

Dahl studied the guard a moment longer, then withdrew. The armed man's presence at least signified the PM was down there . . . somewhere. How to get closer? He might dart across the hall, enter one of the room across there, but that was risky and a safer option had already presented itself.

The door at his side.

Dahl cracked it open and entered the room, praying it had a connecting door exactly like the other he'd seen. This time, luck was on his side. He walked across the room and then the next in total darkness, effectively walking along the corridor towards the guard but without being seen. At the end of the far room, he saw undraped windows looking out over the grounds and a door leading back into the corridor, which, to his guesstimate, stood farther along than the posted guard.

If he looked out the closer door, he just might be able to view along the length of the dogleg.

Dahl checked both guns, one at his waist and one in his hand, and placed his other hand on the doorknob, turning it with more care than he'd ever handled any explosive. Times changed, but the beast was raring to go, barely contained. Dahl wanted to attack, but now would be a foolish time. Pulling the door inward a millimeter at a time, he put an eye to the crack.

Ahead, the dogleg did indeed reveal itself: yet another plush, painting-lined hallway running for at least twenty meters with an enormous bay window at its far end. This particular hallway differed in a big way to all the others.

Armed guards stood along it, one every six feet and on both sides. Some were dressed in suits, others wearing leather jackets and hoodies, every one fidgeting and looking bored. None seemed friendly with the others. Dahl thought they might be rival factions, which made sense, seeing as Grant and Vega would have brought bodyguards along too.

From his restricted vantage point, he couldn't see the door to the room they were guarding, but didn't need to. *No way in there.*

But there was another way.

Retracing his steps back to the bottom of the imagined rectangle, he exited the rooms and returned to the corner around which he'd peered a minute or so earlier. A door stood across the hall, same as before. Logic told him the room was adjoined to the meeting room, and his only way of getting closer. He checked the position of the lone guard, saw him swiping at an Android phone and decided this was as good a time as any.

He leaped across the corridor, a momentary shape, passing quickly. If the guard had looked up, Dahl saw and heard no sign. Waiting for a moment, he opened the door at his back and squeezed into the room, gun ready.

It was a library, hugely impressive with dark oak

bookshelves all packed to the rafters, moveable stepladders and a large table complete with reading light. The overhead light fully illuminated an incongruous single bed tucked away in one corner. Perhaps Sealy worked so hard he could only make it that far at bedtime? Dahl shrugged. To each their own. The most likely scenario was that he frequently ended up blind drunk and then managed to claw his way to the cot.

Wall to wall silence greeted him. If anyone had been in the room, they would surely have frozen. He saw no place to hide and quickly moved over to the connecting door. This time when he put his ear to the polished wood, he immediately picked up the deep timbre of voices.

Footsteps too. Impossible to guess how many men stood or sat on the other side, but it was several. Placing all other concerns aside, he focused on the voices, knowing he would recognize both Vega's and Grant's. The deep Bajan tones and booming laughter probably came from Sealy, but then the unmistakable voice of an Englishman rang out, with quick, rhythmic Spanish-accented English cutting across it.

This was it then. At last.

Dahl had found them, tracked them down. Now only a dozen or so armed guards stood between him and the men who wanted to hurt his family, to pillage Barbados in some clandestine but destructive way, to expand their degenerate empire at the expense of an awful lot of innocent people.

Dahl was so close he could almost smell the rot of the men's souls; like a soiled halo, it hung over the entire house. The problem now was quite concrete, at least, but it did involve a dozen or more soldiers.

With exquisite care, he reached out and checked the interconnecting door to the meeting room.

Locked.

How did he gain surprise entry to a room effectively surrounded by a deep security layer, each man trained to kill and happy to oblige? The problem fizzed around his brain like a mad bull destroying its corral, concentrating all his thoughts on the problem rather than the solution.

Then the penny dropped.

You do it like they'd do it in New York, he thought.

That's *how you do it.*

THIRTY EIGHT

The Facilitator sat with legs crossed, bespoke trousers still showing their creases, both hands on his knees. He presented a sedate figure, easily forgotten, hard to recognize, which still was and always would be his greatest achievement in life.

To date, at any rate. Barbados might just top that . . .

His dealings with Sealy went back a ways, something the Prime Minister never admitted to and no doubt tried to forget. It had been a while since they'd bought the man and then slowly elevated him to this position and, on occasion, he'd thought they would never return to call in their rather large marker. Payday though – it always came sweet to Grant.

He smiled, remembering the sniveling weasel Sealy had been when the Facilitator recognized the opportunity to mold a future tool. Corruption and greed rolled off the man in waves back then – any act, any deal – he'd become a useful machine. Grant had seen the light, or rather the darkness, in Sealy, and helped slough off all the past dealings. He invented a new man. And then went to work. Sealy could bluster and pretend to whomever he wanted, but everyone who mattered knew the stark truth behind it all.

Vega spoke up. "It has not been a good day so far," he spread his hands. "Son lost. Enemy lost. Men to bury. Families to inform. Finally, we come to the reason I am here. It's easy from here on in, Sealy. Do the job you were put here to do. Repay in hard work the funding I gave you."

"Barbados will be the new capital." Sealy smiled. "You have my word."

They owned Sealy and Barbados. Grant had laid the foundations years ago. Sealy was here only to help facilitate a huge increase in the cartel's drug-distribution and money-laundering capabilities, seeing to it that Barbados and its waters became a safe-haven and hub for Vega's international network. From Barbados, product moved easily and efficiently to Europe, North America, and South America. Even Africa, as that still-growing market matured. The island's popular tourist trade made it all work more easily, with Grantley Adams airport handling more than 80 flights a day.

Likewise, when you owned its Prime Minister, Barbados served as the most secure and discreet money-laundering service imaginable. Moving and storing enormous amounts of cash became an eternal albatross for all large-scale narcotics operations. Few cartels had found a solution such as Sealy's small country offered.

Would the island be overrun by the criminal classes and junkies? Grant didn't care. Soon, he'd be moving along to the next job.

The only hitch was that bastard Swede. Grant didn't care that Vega had lost his son and a surprising number of men. He would gladly ignore his own thirst for revenge, if it meant the operation's success. No, Dahl was a problem only because he was a tenacious man and – no matter how isolated – posed a dire threat to the Barbadian operation.

Thoughts of Dahl triggered memories of his family and the Russians. Grant fixed an easy smile on his face but it was merely a Halloween mask, hiding the worst of truths. In reality, he would have traded the entire operation for Dahl chained to a table in a remote location.

"It's time I moved on," he said aloud. "This deal is brokered and now followed to completion. At last," he gave them a perfunctory laugh. "I really don't need to be involved in what comes next."

"Ah, but you should stay." Vega flicked at his suit, removing dust. "One problem remains, does it not?"

Grant glanced around the room, wondering for a moment . . . They sat in the PM's study, a large, square space, dominated by one of the biggest desks Grant had ever seen. A half-full decanter of bourbon sat in pride of place, the amber liquid undulating slightly as Sealy moved.

The PM came around the desk. "Have another drink." He lifted Grant's glass. "The night is long and this moment well anticipated. Where else would you go?" He looked around and let out a deep-toned laugh.

Grant tried to hide his disdain for the man. "You're far from my only client. Name the problem, Gabrio."

"You know his name."

"Ah, well, I know men who can deal with that problem."

Vega looked a little injured. "My men are not good enough?"

Grant remained diplomatic. "Considering all we have worked for and now achieved in Barbados with the Prime Minister, I believe drawing the fight away from here is the best thing to do. Let Dahl alone. Chase us elsewhere if he likes. As we will him. Catch him later."

"Later?"

"A week. A fortnight. A month. Does it really matter, as long as it happens? *Soon.*"

"I looked into his eyes," Sealy said. "He did not scare me. And he could not know the truth."

Grant sighed inwardly. *Nothing quite like having an idiot for a business partner . . .* Now that Vega had lost Vin, dealing with the cartel boss and his allies looked more hazardous than ever.

All the more reason to leave sooner.

Grant doubted Dahl would leave this island before uncovering the truth. Which meant Grant should be long gone already. The undetermined factor here was the knowledge that Dahl couldn't be both soldier and father, the Swede was struggling to switch between both, but the moment that thorny problem solved itself, which it would, Grant expected madness and Armageddon to descend. In that order.

What exactly would Dahl do?

Fight. The Swede would fight. He'd know all the players involved wanted him silenced, so he'd seek to eliminate them. All of them.

Grant experienced a sudden surge of anxiety, looking around the suddenly claustrophobic study. The fact that four of his black-clothed men stood by a couple of Vega's suited thugs didn't help. Sealy's own two bodyguards were there too, stationed at the interconnecting door and the window, hands never more than 50 millimeters from their weapons. Still, the room, while exuding comradeship and success, could easily descend into anarchy at the onset of a bad sneezing fit.

Typical for criminals. They were a hot-tempered lot and one of the many reasons he usually kept them at arm's length. Tonight was unusual for him, the culmination of years of effort.

"You hate Dahl, no?" Vega said. "He might as well have butchered your family himself. Why do you not wish him dead now?"

Grant found it better to say less in these situations. "It feels wiser."

"Wise?" Vega shrugged. "Wise is destroying the man from my office, a digital keystroke at a time. What we did today was not wise. It was revenge ruled by the heart, not the head. If we let him go now . . ." Vega sighed.

Grant drained half his bourbon. "He's in the wind, Gabrio. The trackers are gone. What do you suggest?"

The hidden fury deep within Vega simmered a little, betrayed by a subtle tightening of his jawline over the hard gaze.

"I pay *you* to suggest and to win." Vega said. "Where are your *cojones*? Are you not the man who organized the tracking down of the very same Russians who murdered your wife and child? Are you not the man who dictated every torture visited upon them? Even in prison? Have you forgotten?"

"I am that man, and I never forget," he answered softly. "Never."

Vega opened his arms. "There you go. So Dahl dies, tonight. Agreed?"

Oh, of course, just let me pull his lily-white, Scandinavian arse out of my jacket pocket and we're all done, you two-faced son-of-a-bitch.

"Not a problem," he said. "I do believe we should get right to it."

"Hey, what's the rush?" Sealy protested with dull appreciation of the problem at hand. "This is the good shit, you know? The best shit on the island. I've come a long way from Long Bay, have I not? Ha ha. Drink up, gentlemen. To us!"

So Sealy was becoming drunker by the minute and Vega was having delusions of invincibility. The armed guards looked bored. Grant feigned another sip of bourbon, using the opportunity to check his watch.

The clock was ticking.

THIRTY NINE

Dahl turned off the reading light, allowed his eyes to adjust to the darkness and listened to the house, in particular the corridor outside. He'd thought about it a dozen ways and, yes, there was a way to get in that room. Not a particularly elegant way, but then his enemies would only be disappointed by refinement.

Most high-story burglaries and home invasions in New York City occurred only because people left their lofty windows open or unlocked. To exploit that weakness, thieves often came down from the roof.

It was similar here. Despite all the security, with its seemingly invulnerable top-floor setting, the library window was unlocked. Dahl took this as a good sign that the room next door would follow suit. He'd noted earlier that the Prime Minister's residence had many windows overlooking narrow balconies. Dahl cracked the window, scanning the grounds as he worked. The pent-up anxieties of prowling through the old house manifested as stomach acid, making him pull a face but not stopping him from hanging his head out of the window, a blonde gargoyle seeking sanctuary. Sure enough, a balcony was affixed to the room next door. Good fortune. The downside was that it hung too far away to make the jump even reasonably possible. He'd be gambling with his life. To complicate matters, a pool of light flooded from the window, revealing that – like the library's window – it lacked a covering.

Nobody said it'd be as easy as invading a small country. Get on with it. That guard could be awake by now.

Dahl stood back, refusing to give up, recognizing the

chance that presented itself tonight, wondering if a more characteristic assault might actually be the way to go.

All in. Balls out. Head on. Brain off.

That's when another way presented itself and, as Dahl walked towards it, a plan B. He stripped the library's small bed of sheets and the pillows of their cases, tied them all together with as much vigor as he could muster and returned to the window. Quickly, he extended one leg outside, then the other, now perching on the sill more than ten meters above the ground. This was no time to stop and admire the view, as the men stationed below would surely spot him. It was time to go ballistic. He attached one end of the knotted sheets to the radiator under the library window and pulled. Nothing moved.

He jumped out into empty space.

But not too far. Holding onto the improvised rope, he positioned himself with feet flat against the vertical wall and began to crab across to the next balcony. No shouts went up from below.

You see: luck evens out in the end.

Without exerting too much effort, Dahl reached the next balcony and pulled himself up to the railing. Quickly, he tied the sheet off so that it wouldn't swing away, then hauled himself over, making sure he stayed out of the window's direct line-of-sight. A fast glance showed a man standing, feet-apart, inside the window, staring into the room but blocking Dahl's view.

That might actually work for me.

Dahl shifted down low and carefully peered between the guy's open legs, quickly scanning the entire room. Not everything was visible, but the scene convinced him that it was now or never. Still, the spiky question remained:

How?

It was a large room, inhabited by at least six guards, many more in the hallway through the door, and Dahl's three targets. A cop stood among them too, a cartoon grin stretched across his face. Maybe the bastard was high.

Dahl withdrew, put his back to the wall, and thought about it. Years of training, hard drill and field experience flickered through his thoughts, helpful sparks in a conflagration of uncertainty, as time ticked away.

You have moments, not days. What would . . . what would . . .

"What would the Mad Swede do?" he asked aloud.

Yell 'fuck it' and charge, he knew. But that wasn't the answer. In the end, the answer was easy and presented itself from unknown depths.

Easy.

You draw them out.

FORTY

Johanna huddled with her children, Dario at their side. With time to catch up, to reflect, it was surprising to her that she fought against the new change in her, at least at first. After a moment she realized that this *new* Johanna now occupied the driving seat and she wanted to keep that Johanna for as long as her kids were in danger.

Sensible move. If today had taught her anything, it was that people could change. She'd do well to remember that when Torsten returned and, later, they got chance to discuss their marriage. This nightmare wasn't over yet, though.

Dario nudged her, saying nothing. She raised her head from where she'd been nuzzling Isabella's hair and listening to the quiet murmurs of her steady breathing. She followed Dario's gaze along the beach and back towards the road, where buildings lined the boundary.

Shadows were abroad in the night, impossible to discern at this distance, but suspicious in the way they moved and crept in silence. This wasn't a night to be rash. She untangled herself from her daughters and inched over to Dario.

"It's them."

"How do you know?"

Johanna shrugged, smiling quickly as Isabella raised a questioning head. "I don't. But do you want to risk it?"

"I'm not sure what we can do. If we move we risk alerting them, and—" Dario paused as Johanna put a hand on his arm.

"I've been thinking about taking some initiative. Finding a cell or landline and calling up the cavalry. My husband's colleagues," she clarified. "If they don't know where we are . . . what my husband's doing . . . We don't want any 'friendly-fire' incidents."

Dario nodded, but his face looked pale and drawn. "I'm not doing so well," he murmured, pointing to his shoulder while also trying to keep the movement hidden. "This feels worse."

Johanna squinted hard. "The bleeding hasn't stopped," she said. "Do you feel bad?"

"A little . . . woozy."

"Shit," Johanna murmured under her breath. The searchers had changed tack and were now skirting the rear of the buildings, heading toward them in a big loop. A decision had to be made, and she wished for a moment that Torsten were here to do it. *No. Don't think that way.* She had to stay strong. This was a good hiding place, but it was also a discoverable one. Skimming through her earlier thoughts, it made sense to get away from what seemed to be a search that was closing in on them. Move away from here to make that communication to Dahl's colleagues. For all their sakes.

That left Dario. She wouldn't leave him or send him on his way. Instead, she leaned in until the cloying reek of fresh blood filled her nostrils and examined the bandage.

Soaked through. She was no nurse, but she thought a larger bandage, tied the same way, might help. The initial bandage would serve as packing. Turning, she shushed Julia's protests and tore the sleeve away from her daughter's thin cardigan. Then she silenced Dario with a look and wrapped the material tightly around the other bandage, pushing it hard against the wound.

"Pressure," she explained in a whisper.

Dario bit his lip, piercing the skin and drawing blood.

"Don't make a sound," she said in his ear.

She wound it more tightly, twisting the ends, tourniquet-style, each small revolution compressing the wound until the old bandage could no longer be seen. Then she tied it off.

"I'm sorry," she said. "It's not great but it should help. And we're about out of time."

Dario nodded again, clearly suffering but already using the fence at his back to rise. Johanna did the same and helped her kids to their feet. As one, they melded with the darkness, wishing it would encompass them, bury them deep in its black maw. The searchers hadn't roamed far, but were still advancing, as relentless as the approaching dawn. If they didn't move now they would end up trapped with only the sea at their backs.

Johanna urged Dario ahead at a steady pace. They hugged the fence, aiming for an alley that speared through the buildings ahead. Essentially, Johanna thought, if they could escape detection as the searchers passed by and then return to the same spot they were home and dry. Safe. Not even these men had the resources to search everywhere twice.

And, using the time they had, she hoped to find a cell phone.

Their pace had to increase though, if they were to escape detection. Avoiding tufts of grass, heaps of garbage and treading the uneven sand didn't help. Isabella fell once, but Johanna caught her and, with Julia's help, managed to keep her from crying out.

Julia put a finger to her sister's lips as tears welled. "It's okay, little one. Be brave and follow me."

Johanna found herself fighting tears too. Fear assaulted her gut like a trapped bird, fighting for release. But no, that was the one thing she couldn't allow. She'd be signing four death warrants.

No. Five.

They crouched low. They forged ahead, not pausing to rest. They needed to change their situation – rather than leave anything to chance. Dario reached the edge of the beach first and paused.

Johanna gauged the hunters. They were still some way off, shrouded, but even the slightest noise might alert them out here. Nothing else stirred, nothing to help mask their presence. Johanna saw heads casting from side to side, arms holding the shapes of weapons. Her heart hammered. The sand slipped beneath her as she urged Isabella and Julia forward, straight into the alley. Dario waited until Johanna passed and then joined them.

"Quickly," he urged. "Watch the floor."

Johanna moved ahead, treading lightly but swiftly now, trying to get out of range. Something rustled among garbage to her right as she scooted by. It was only a matter of minutes before she heard a yell at their backs.

"Hey! Thought I heard something down here."

She froze, then herded everyone against the dank, high wall, crouching down to take advantage of the deeper darkness at ground level.

Flashlights cut a swathe towards them. Huge shadow-figures lumbered behind them.

"See anything?" a guttural voice asked.

"Nah . . . oh, wait."

The beams joined. A hammer clicked. A stick-thin cat, disturbed by the bright light, dashed away, a dead rat dangling from its mouth. Laughter filled the alley.

Rough words were passed, and finally a man said: "You scare like a girl, mon. Come on, we got work to do."

Johanna let out a deep breath as the men moved on, but didn't stand on ceremony. They had ridden their luck there, just a little.

"Nasty kitty," Isabella said.

Johanna had to agree, but it was certainly a survivor. Like them. That, she could respect.

She led them further though the narrow darkness until

they approached its far end. Once there, she stopped and viewed the way ahead as best she could without revealing any part of her body.

Traveling on the winds came the beating sound of carnival, the whoops of laughter and cries of surprise. The party was still going, still flamboyantly loud. Closer, she heard the rattle of a can skimming along the road, the tap-tap of branches knocking against a window. There were no people around – tourist, locals, or cops. Everyone either seemed to be attending the parade or already wrapped up in bed.

But another idea had occurred to her. This was largely a business district, interspersed with a few pubs and civilian homes. If she couldn't pickpocket a resident and be sure to get away with it, surely she could find a quiet, working landline.

She saw an abundance of square-shaped opportunities, some with rusted bars on the windows and others with enormous padlocks hanging from flimsy looking doors. Another problem struck her. *I can't leave the kids, even with Dario.*

The mere concept was as alien as a flying saucer. She eyed the alleyway behind them. It stood perfectly quiet now and offered a path of refuge back to the beach. They would have to hurry.

"Take this," she stooped down and handed Dario a large piece of ragged masonry.

"Why?"

She gestured across the street, at the small building with the lightest padlock. "We need to use their phone."

"Are you kidding me?" Dario shifted uncomfortably, holding the shoulder wound tenderly.

"I won't let my husband down." Johanna said. "I may . . . may . . ." She didn't add 'never see him again' for the sake of the kids.

"How can this help?" Dario didn't look convinced.

"We warn the incoming team. Tell them where Torsten is. Where we are. You don't want to get shot by our saviors do you? We find out how much longer we have to wait."

"Well, that sounds sensible actually. All right, give me a minute."

Dario steeled himself, checked the vicinity, and then marched quickly across the road. As he paused by the padlock, Johanna took hold of the girls' hands and pulled them along with her. It was both a blessing and a curse that they'd passed that point of exhaustion now, and gave no voice of complaint.

Dario smashed the lock. Johanna cast glances in every direction. No alarm sounded, but she hadn't imagined it would in this poorer part of town. The door led to an office, which housed an untidy desk. Dario pointed at the large piece of black plastic.

"There you go."

Johanna didn't waste time. She asked Dario to hunt around for food and water for the kids while she dialed, aware that they could be discovered or reported at any moment. In the end, the younger Vega came up with a stash of bottom-drawer chocolate bars and an unopened can of cola. He shrugged doubtfully.

"Are you kidding?" Johanna said. "That's perfect."

A coarse voice with an odd accent suddenly answered the phone: "Yeah, who's this?"

She knew the speaker. "It's Johanna. We don't have long."

"Gotcha. Go ahead."

Johanna collected her thoughts in a hurry. "The highlights – both Grant and Vega are here to do business with Prime Minister Sealy, not to kill him, as it first appeared. Torsten said they own him. And they're doing their business right now. We'll be on Pebbles Beach, somewhere near the Harbour Lights club. And they still have men out there searching for us."

"We'll come in hard," the man said. "But, tell me love, why isn't Dahl making this call?"

"He's gone to sort it all out."

A restrained snort from the other end. "Of course he has. And you, you're safe? Unhurt?"

"Yes. We will be." She didn't have time to tell them all about Dario. "How long will you be?"

"Not long. Less than an hour. Do you have Dahl's location?"

Johanna explained about the PM's residence and Dahl's idea. She left the final plea unspoken, because the man she talked to wanted to save her husband just as much as she did.

"We'll come for you first," he said. "And then the residence. If anything changes try to let me know."

Johanna confirmed, hung up, and then looked Dario in the eye. "Time to go. We've done all we can."

"Are you sure going back to the beach is the best idea?"

"It's a great hiding place, and it should be safer still once they've already checked it. What could be better?"

"I hear ya."

Johanna took hold of the girls' hands, grabbed a bit of chocolate, and led them back toward the street.

The words sounded great, but she was a sapling bending in the midst of a storm. A stronger sapling than yesterday, but bendable and breakable nonetheless.

"Where are we going, Mummy?" Isabella asked.

"The beach, darling. You know how you like the beach."

"Not today." The quiet retort.

Just one more hour, Johanna thought. *Please just give us that.*

FORTY ONE

Dahl's improvised sheet-rope wasn't long enough. Not even close. He did see that he could make a safe jump to the ground, but that was missing the point – there were two halves to this plan. Dahl decided to take a little time and dial the risk ratio to full. He backtracked, retracing his steps to the housecleaner he'd tied up in the unoccupied bedroom and gathered up the bedding linens she'd been carrying. Time slipped away, but not too fast now that he knew where he was going and exactly what he was doing. And if the original guard had recovered by now – it hardly mattered. A general alarm is what he was after.

Dahl used the now-lengthened sheet-rope to abseil all the way to the ground and left it dangling. Funny thing, when you wanted to catch a criminal's attention, you just couldn't get a bloody break. No warning shouts, not even a challenge split the night air as he dangled off the side of the residence, hit the ground, or began moving heedlessly around the house.

Time to change it up a bit.

Now on a different side of the mansion from where his rope still hung, Dahl sought the closest window and broke it with the butt of his pistol. Glass smashed, shouts filled the air. At last men came forth, some flicking cigarette butts as they ran, others hastily pocketing cell phones. One fell over a tree branch. That would be Vega's contribution, then.

Dahl ensured he was spotted by multiple men, then ran steadily back the way he'd come. Radios squawked. Protocol would dictate the guards chase and apprehend, but Dahl knew the caliber of the men up in that room.

Maybe they'd guess it was he, maybe they didn't care a jot, but the order would soon come down – shoot to kill.

Dahl ran hard. A man appeared ahead, sprinting the other way. Their eyes locked, the man's gaze hardening. Dahl used his momentum to leap high, elbow pointed down. As the two men came together in their crude joust, Dahl slammed down with faultless accuracy, landing the point of his elbow on the man's cheekbone and driving him to his knees. For his part, the guard rammed a heavy fist into Dahl's ribs. Tensed muscle absorbed most of the blow, focus diverting the pain. The Mad Swede didn't break stride, leaving the guard in his wake, approaching the corner of the house and spotting his sheet-rope still hanging toward the back. Now it was vital to stay ahead. The crackle of radios sounded like maddened birds whizzing all around, the warning yells white noise, pointless. It wouldn't be long until—

The first shot rang out, the bullet smashing into the wall to Dahl's left, producing a plume of mortar and brick dust. He sprinted with everything he had until, reaching the sheet-rope, he took hold and planted both feet against the wall.

Time to . . .

"Hold it, asshole. You ain't fuckin' Spiderman so get the hell down from there."

Dahl didn't think, just thrust and threw himself backwards from the wall in the direction of the voice. His body struck the guy, who grunted and staggered. Dahl managed to regain his balance and spin—

Only to be hit by a sledgehammer; the man's head angled down, shoulders out, slamming into Dahl's gut and knocking the wind right out of him. Dahl held on as he was propelled backwards, then dug his heels in, the edges churning up dirt as he sought to deplete the power in the charge. The man soon came to a halt and tried to back away, but Dahl heaved on the downturned shoulders, raising the man's heels off the ground. The guard acted like he'd never known the like of it before, kicking like a mule and shaking his head like a rabid dog. Dahl clapped both sides of his head with open palms.

The man staggered. "What the fuck *are* you?"

Dahl gritted his teeth rather than reply. No point wasting breath. Gathering power, he took hold of the man with two hands, hefted his bulk and then threw him around and against the wall. Unable to stop it, tumbling in mid-air, the hefty guard tried to curl fetal ahead of the impact. Dahl growled and stomped at the man, but the guard rolled away from his foot. He rose to a knee, visibly trying to clear his head but incredibly still holding onto the gun.

"Really?" With regret, Dahl broke the arm and threw the gun, leaving the man writhing. It was the only way. With seconds to spare, he returned to the wall and started to climb, feet and hands moving triple-time.

Dahl hauled himself up and over the balcony once more and drew both guns.

FORTY TWO

The balcony was clear, the room beyond standing as expected – less crowded. Vega at least would have sent extra men to assess the danger, thus thinning out the guards.

So far, so good.

He stepped through the balcony doors, guns leveled, a man alone against eight or nine and liking his chances. He'd faced worse and sent every offender plummeting down to that special place reserved for them beneath Satan's toilet. The first guard to spot him coming through the window drew. Dahl shot him between the eyes, covering the next man in blood and worse. A second guard missed that memo and also tried to line Dahl up, falling a moment later with a brand-new, smoking eye in his forehead. Vega and Prime Minister Sealy were standing, immobile, still trying to register that guns were pointed at their heads. Other hands moved to weapons but Dahl shook his head.

"Don't."

Indecision froze the room. Some men had already drawn weapons but now held them pointed at the floor.

Dahl didn't waste time. Others would arrive and change the dynamic. He waved the barrel of a gun, bunching the guards together, and then raised an eyebrow at Vega.

"Where's Grant?"

"Gone. A few minutes ago."

The man was slipperier than engine oil. Bunching the guards together had probably been a mistake, but then he could hardly leave them apart. Lowered guns itched to be raised and Dahl fought to watch every single one.

"You are outnumbered," Vega pointed out.

"And how did that work out for you last time?" Dahl kept his eyes on the armed men. "If I see one barrel rise, I will shoot two men. That's a lot of tears and funerals, Gabrio."

"They're not all my men."

"How about you, Sealy? Your boys get life insurance? Dental?"

"Dahl," Vega interrupted. "What are you going to do?"

"Take away everyone's reason for being here," he said, still not looking at the cartel boss. "You. I'm taking you."

"Torsten . . ." Vega began, then abruptly changed tack. "One million for the man who shoots him first. *One million dollars!*"

Dahl tightened his grip, his eyes sweeping the room. Barrels swayed, raised and lowered. Fingers twitched. A true standoff. Vega's men were perhaps a bit reticent, knowing they had jobs for life; Sealy's men danced on the edge. All knew that many of their colleagues had tested Dahl and failed.

"Don't," Dahl warned softly. "Don't."

Men shifted. Dahl almost fired. He held off, knowing a single shot would start a bloodbath in which all could die. The strain smothered him, the tension tauter than a guy-wire. Vega and Sealy appeared nonplussed, unsure what form of leadership was required next.

Dahl wondered where Grant was. The man was as cautious as a snake and Dahl doubted Vega would know. He could press the question but that would only waste time. "The balcony, Vega."

"Oh, and then we can go?" Vega asked. "Sure."

"Last chance."

"Men are on their way, asshole. This is *your* last chance."

Dahl judged the room. "This bastard offered one of you a million dollars to shoot me," he said. "Ain't you gonna collect?"

And he moved, sidestepping toward the desk and Vega as one of the men snapped and drew. Dahl's gun exploded first, a bullet penetrating the offender's right bicep and drawing out a heavy groan. Dahl switched his tactics and pointed one gun at Vega's throat, now less than a foot away.

"Come here."

"Fuck you. Shoot him."

But nobody dared risk it. None held sufficient belief in his own skillset to risk the shot.

He reached down to the desk and grabbed a letter opener. Before anyone could react, he rammed it through the top of Vega's hand, pinning it to the desk. "Last chance. Come now." Escaping alive meant he had to take Vega with him.

Vega stifled a scream, but vented with a string of curses, punctuated with information. "*Pendejo!* Where will you take me? You go quickly. I will let you leave. You had best look after your family now!"

Dahl drew a breath, taking stock. The gun never wavered. He almost wished one of these assholes would make a move so he could blow Vega's head off. But the cartel boss's statement shed a different light on things.

You had best look after your family now.

His family waited far away from here. But Grant had left some minutes ago. Could the Facilitator know where they were hiding? Hazard a guess? Grant knew Dahl well, and he'd hunted them across the island for a day or more. But surely . . .

Dario.

"How?" he managed. "Just . . . fucking . . . *how?*"

"You think devices can only be put in watches and bracelets?" Vega spat, then shrugged. "Well, sometimes that is true. But family? We are *skin deep.* Yes?" Vega laughed. "Grant has my tracker with him."

Dahl reacted instantly, before anyone could speak or even blink. He unfastened Vega from the desk by yanking on the man's wrist, pulling away the injured hand and letter opener together, then swept a thick arm around the man's throat and wielded both guns at once, barrels pointed outward, covering the room with a steady, roving scan.

"We're leaving," he said. "Anyone brave enough to take a shot better have perfect aim."

Shoving the drug lord along, Dahl contracted behind the man's frame, manipulating his walk to maintain maximum cover. He passed Sealy, leaving himself wide open to the man. He expected the Prime Minister possessed little or no personal courage, which proved correct as Vega openly urged the man to act and received only a hooded frown in return.

"I will gut you personally after this." Vega growled at Sealy.

Dahl pushed him toward the room's hallway door, not wanting to complicate the situation any further. Time to call last orders on this particular party. Hardened gazes sought his, looking for an opening. Fingers still twitched, and Dahl challenged every one, the Mad Swede communicating with his eyes the essential truth of the situation.

"They were right," Vega said. "You are mad."

Dahl nodded at the five men he left behind, the four lined up along the wall outside and the one stationed at the end of the corridor. "You wouldn't recognize a set of proper balls if they slapped you in the face, Gabrio," he said loudly. Then more quietly, "Proof of that lies in your son."

"Easy to say from behind a gun," Vega said. "So what would you do, Mad One? What would you do if you were them?" He indicated his own men.

Dahl leaned in close. "Easy. I'd shoot you in the gut, then me in the head."

They neared the end of the first hall, the man there backing away, arms actually upraised. Clearly, he didn't understand the situation. Not that Dahl minded. He urged Vega onward, over to the second-floor landing and then downstairs. Another bunch of guards and mercs waited in the lobby, calculating angles and risks, but Dahl remained in constant motion and manipulated Vega around slightly at every step, always changing the viewpoints and positions, always fluid. Still, he brandished both guns simultaneously, making himself as threatening a figure as they'd ever seen. Not once did the soldier in him fail, not once did the strength and focus acquired from years of training and battle deteriorate. The air outside struck him like a cold towel, much welcomed. He inched his captive over to the row of parked cars and stopped along the path, breathing steadily.

"Keys!" he called out.

"Duh," one of Vega's men returned. "Already inside."

Dahl regarded the man, his bullet head and Goofy ears, his skew-whiff tie and uncomfortable-looking suit. "Where do you find 'em?" he asked Vega.

The Mexican nodded. "On this we can agree," he muttered. "But they are my blood now. My clan. It is complicated."

Dahl opened the door and pushed Vega in first, following the man like a patch of glue, sticking to him right across the front of the car. Vega fell into the driver's seat and Dahl settled alongside.

"Drive."

Vega turned the key and the engine roared to life.

Dahl struggled with the frustration and buckled up. "Now go."

The car moved off, tires crunching as it left the concrete and turned onto the gravel drive. Vega juiced the throttle and watched Dahl, who motioned toward the upcoming gates. "Watch the road. Drive safe."

"Oh, yes, Miss Daisy." Vega slowed as the gates slid aside and then pulled out onto the badly lit road. Passing traffic was non-existent at this time of night. Dahl swiveled to check the rear view.

"Here they come."

"What? You think they just let us go? They're not stupid; they know you won't shoot me as I drive."

"Well, you got half of that right."

Vega blinked. "Which half?"

Dahl ignored him and watched the road ahead, wary of Vega's driving and those in pursuit. Each vehicle looked identical – black Lincolns with privacy glass all around and dull rims –the two following Dahl being driven more than a little enthusiastically.

Vega took a curve at speed, accelerating through it.

Dahl waved the gun. "Slow down."

"Don't you want to escape them?"

"I want to arrive in one piece."

"Then maybe you should not have stabbed me, *puto*." Vega gunned the engine, aiming for the side of the road.

Dahl had almost forgotten the letter opener in Vega's hand. With a long-suffering sigh, he grabbed the steering wheel and held it straight with one hand, countering Vega's lesser strength, much to the Mexican's vexation, and holding the gun steady with the other.

"Stop acting like a child," he said. "And just drive."

Vega sprang at him, the rage taking hold, the wheel forgotten. His blind anger lent him brute strength. A blow flew past Dahl's defenses, striking his skull and knocking the other side of his head against the window. The same hand struck again with less force, right above Dahl's eye, causing a lightning flash of pain. Dahl leaned across and righted the wheel as the car drifted, ignoring his irate captive for the moment. A third punch landed, rendered weak by the lack of space in the front of the car.

Dahl set the car on course and sat back. "Are you finished?"

"Fuck you! *Fuck you!*" In his temper, Vega wrenched the letter-opener free and turned it upon his captor. Dahl caught the descending wrist and twisted until the letter opener fell to the carpet.

Cars zoomed up close in the rear view mirror.

Shit. This is getting out of hand.

Time to rein it all in.

Dahl twisted Vega's wrist to snapping point, draining all the fight out of the man. "*Drive*. Foot on the pedal," he said. "Or the letter opener goes in the other hand."

Vega complied, nursing his wrist like it was a childhood pet, eyes glued to the road. Dahl twisted, aimed one of the pistols, and blew the back window out.

Glass shattered, air roared inside the car. Vega slewed the wheels. Dahl watched the chase vehicles, smiling grimly when the first skidded and then ran off the road, bouncing down a verge and slamming fender-first into the bottom of a ditch. It hit so hard the back-end shuddered and slid, almost toppling over. Dahl fixed his eyes upon the second vehicle. It raced up to them now, lights as bright as exploding planets, engine wailing under pressure. Vega took a tight turn at speed. Dahl estimated they were no more than ten minutes from the beach and quickly gave Vega directions. The pursuit car blasted up alongside, its passenger now eyeballing Vega and trying to aim his weapon at Dahl.

"You know," Dahl said, "they really should shoot the tires. Or the engine."

"Not all men were brought up eating Marine dirt," Vega muttered.

Dahl silenced him by aiming behind Vega's head and pulling the trigger. The bullet parted hairs before it crashed through the other car, hitting the driver and making it slide and veer into an unstoppable tumble, side over side until it finally stopped, wheels up.

"Actually, I went to an expensive English university. Until they kicked me out."

Vega nodded as if everything he saw and heard made perfect sense. "Why'd they kick you out?"

Dahl wasn't surprised when the smile came instantly, but he did try to hide it. "You've met her."

"Seriously, I don't care. You destroyed years of planning and investment today. Years."

"No," Dahl replied. "You did that when you decided to take me and my family on. Turn left up ahead."

Vega slowed, took the turn, and then headed for the parking area that Dahl indicated. "Never," he said.

Dahl looked at him. "What?"

"Never."

"Look, just park there and shut the fu—"

Vega hit the gas pedal, deliberately crashing the car into a parked van. Dahl jerked forward. Vega jumped him again, striking at Dahl with both hands. "You'll *never* . . . take me . . . alive!"

This time, Dahl had no patience. The clock was ticking and Grant had already been out of sight for too long. Johanna and the children were vulnerable. As Vega pounced, the Mad Swede met him head on, forehead down, teeth bared. Vega's face impacted hard with the unbreakable wall, nose breaking, lips mashing and tearing, eye-socket cracking. As he yelped, Dahl ended it abruptly with a devastating punch fueled by fury, right between the Mexican's eyes.

"I should kill you. Stay down."

Vega did.

Why not kill him now?

It was the particular line he didn't like to cross. Vega was nicely immobilized, out of it for a while. Situation anesthetized; don't make it worse.

Dahl pocketed the gun and looked around the car. There was nothing with which to restrain Vega and he wasn't about to let the man off the leash this time. Again, the extent of his plight hit home – he wore swim-shorts and stolen trainers; not even a belt to tie up the murderous Mexican. Not wanting to waste one more second, Dahl exited the car, grabbed Vega by the hair and pulled him into the street.

"Stay with me," he said. "You run, I'll shoot you in the gut."

"Whatever, *cabrón*. I treat my men better than you treat your captives."

Dahl didn't even try to decipher that kind of thinking. It bordered on the entryway to the nuthouse. He pressed through the parking area to the very back and the place where he knew a gap in the fence existed . . . the beach beyond.

No sounds interrupted them. No tell-tale whispers or scrapes in the dark. The night arced above and the stars glittered their magic. This area of Barbados was as quiet as the grave as Torsten Dahl led Gabrio Vega, the boss of one of the world's most brutal cartels, in search of Nick Grant, the loathsome facilitator of some of the worst crimes ever perpetrated on humanity.

Dahl wanted so badly to be wrong about Grant's intentions. Almost wished his vile stain had left the country.

But it hadn't.

FORTY THREE

Dahl moved like a nimble wraith, at home in the shadows, chasing one insanity while dragging another along at his side. Vega didn't protest, stepping as well as he could. Dahl paused as he entered the tree-line and then studied the beach beyond. Swathed in darkness, he could actually make out very little but dark shapes, darker mounds, and the swell of the ocean in the distance. Waves lapped at the shore. A fetid stench of rotting undergrowth and litter competed with the salty air. He swept the area with an experienced gaze.

"Wait."

He stayed absolutely still. Even when he knew exactly where Johanna, the kids and Dario were, he could not see them. That set his heart to beating faster. The fatherly panic reared up, but he forced it down.

Not now. Please, not now.

Half a minute passed and a tiny shape moved. That would be Isabella. All was well. Dahl broke cover, urged Vega along and headed in their general direction. Still, he didn't trust the darkness, the shadows. If Grant truly had taken the GPS receiver tracking Dario from Vega, why would he . . .

Dahl paused.

"Why did you send Grant?" he whispered to Vega. "Why him?"

Vega's eyes lit up with the knowledge of a well-kept secret. "Because Grant wants you dead. You. Not your family. *You*. And he has the best motivation."

Dahl didn't see it coming until it smashed him on the head. Literally. Grant flew out of the darkness, a weapon raised, and brought it crashing down onto Dahl, sending him to his knees in the sand.

"He was waiting for *you*." Vega grinned. "Not your family." Grant threw Vega a weapon, something long and rusty and raggedly sharp.

Dahl bled from the temple. Midnight swirled around his head, blurring all focus. The sand shifted beneath him, but it wasn't the sand, he realized. It was his equilibrium, stretching from dazed to woozy. Grant hadn't survived and thrived so long by being stupid, so he came at Dahl again while he was down. The weapon swung from on high, this time striking Dahl's substantial shoulder, generating pain in spears that branched off and ran the length of his body. Dahl cried out and fell sideways, grabbing his shoulder, blinded by agony. Vega suddenly came to intensely animated life, saying something about taking revenge for his men and their families.

"My wife? Her name was Sarah." The Facilitator spoke from above him. "Sarah Green. Hell, she was a firecracker at school. Teased all the boys." He bent over to whisper into Dahl's ear. "But I won her. She was *mine.*"

Another swing of the weapon – Dahl guessed it to be a length of iron pipe – and fire erupted along the top on his back, just below his neck. Still woozy, he wobbled, held up by one hand scrabbling around in the sand.

"My daughter? Michelle. Also *mine.*"

Dahl knew it was coming. Grant, despite his own experience, couldn't resist the revenge speech, now that he was on top. Dahl rolled forward as the pipe came down, missing the brunt of the blow, the movement making him even more light-headed. Blood poured from his head to the thirsty sand.

Grant drew his frame upright, maybe realizing he'd lost some control. Vega jumped in and drove two kicks into Dahl's back, now brandishing the length of broken railing. Grant upended the iron pipe so that its jagged point aimed downwards.

"Right through," Vega encouraged him. "Send it right through one side and out the other."

"*Father?*" A young male voice then spoke out. "You killed the woman I loved, and tried to have me killed. Now I return the favor."

Dario came out of the pitch-black beach, an avenging dark-angel, gun raised, and swung a rock. The weapon struck Vega on the top of the skull, sent him spinning, and made Grant lunge away. Dario's second swipe missed its mark, and then he was leaping after his father, bending down to take up the discarded length of broken railing, catching his father and driving it into the back of his neck as both men staggered.

Vega gurgled in the sand, blood leaking from his body, painting the beach only with a deeper darkness at this hour. He reached up a shaking hand.

"Make sure . . . make sure . . ." he rattled. "They give me a good . . . send-off."

The delusions of power, of leadership, of money. They never ceased and they were never less than ocean deep.

Dahl had used the time to hold still, to grab his spinning head and make the world normal again. Pain still lanced all his nerve endings, but the faintness had passed. He shuffled around in the sand now as he heard the empty clicking of Dario's gun.

The Facilitator took the opportunity to launch his final, deadly attack.

Dahl rose as Grant descended, grabbed the wrist that held the pipe and helped the man on his way, flinging him over his head. Dahl crabbed around as quickly as he could, moaning at the pain. Grant had landed on his back and rolled, and now he came up swinging. A snarl made a rictus of his features as he used the jagged pipe end as a sword tip, stabbing fast – two, three times. Dahl shifted slightly each time, working from his knees and doing his best to allow the pipe to pass him by, turning at the last moment, using the passing time to regain his strength.

Grant only tried harder, clearly knowing he could only defeat Dahl while the Mad Swede remained weakened by injury.

It almost looked absurd – the suited Englishman fencing with the pipe. But Dahl could not underestimate Grant. This was the man who'd taken out the main contingent of the Russian mob that had slaughtered his wife and child. This was the man who'd held governments for ransom and initiated coups. He wouldn't go gently.

And he had reason to fight, as good as Dahl's.

Grant struck again. Dahl used the moment to spring to a standing position. The pipe scraped down his arm, but it didn't matter. He'd regained his feet, forcing Grant to circle. A few puny stabs elicited no reaction from Dahl, but when he circled around to where he could lay eyes upon his family – his concentration broke.

Grant sprang. The pipe hit again, swinging across Dahl's neck, leaving a three-inch gash but luckily not breaking a critical blood vessel. Nothing serious, Dahl knew, but again he'd been undone by the nearness of kin.

Hoping Johanna turned the girls' heads away, Dahl moved into Grant's next swing, dropped a shoulder and hurled the man into the air. Grant landed hard, but came up quick, kicking out and striking with double jabs.

"Look at you, trying to fight. Thought you were just a back-room pussy."

"Trained by the best," Grant said. "Akia Dojo. I'll sell your girls to them when we're done."

Dahl smiled. These people, they learned from black belts and thought they were Bruce Lee. Maybe they were, but Bruce Lee wasn't Torsten Dahl.

Grant danced in like Tinkerbell, all elbows, knees and squeals. Dahl let him have the first two hits, then trapped the sword arm, elbowed his nose and caught hold of Grant's neck. He twisted. Grant started to buck, realizing his mistake. Dahl let him wriggle free to gain an even better position, then blazed his own path of utter destruction on the man who wanted to kill his family. Four strikes in lightning-quick procession stunned Grant, brought blood and tears and teeth falling, and left the man standing, staring into space, mind blown, no doubt wondering why the hell his sensei hadn't warned him what a military man could do.

"Dojo this," Dahl said, landing a simple kick never seen in any Van Damme movie. Grant collapsed to the sand, unconscious.

Breathing hard, Dahl glanced over at the motionless Dario. "Come here, mate. Come with me."

The lad was staring at his dying father, regret mixed with fear and anger in his eyes. Dahl saw resolve there too, and hoped he might use it to absorb and process the brutal killing of his girlfriend. Such things could never be left behind, but they could be lived with, at least during the daylight hours.

"For now," Dahl said, "I'd like to have you join my family."

He stepped away a few strides, mindful of Grant's current blackout and potential revival, but unable to stay away from his daughters for one more second.

"Isabella," he breathed. "Julia."

The smiles on their faces washed it all away, hours of unimaginable stress and horror and anxiety sloughing away to reveal the new skin beneath.

"Turns out I'm not only a soldier," he said.

Johanna came with them for the family huddle. "I've missed you, Torsten, and not just tonight. I guess the soldier can be useful though."

"Is everyone okay?"

"I think so. It's early days." She attempted a smile.

Dahl let them in, hugged them close and thought about the great change he'd seen in his wife today. No longer did she run within the pack. Now she owned the pack.

"You took it beyond the limit today. And helping the team out like that . . ." he paused, impressed and sorry he hadn't seen it in her before. "

"And you're surprised?" Johanna smiled lightly, as if the whole thing had been entirely expected and natural.

"Not at all." Dahl bowed his head.

Sirens split the night all around them, police cars streaming along the road and pulling into the car park. Dahl looked over at the motionless body of Gabrio Vega and the unconscious form of Nick Grant, watched over by Dario. How would this change things?

Where was Sealy?

Would this day ever end?

FORTY FOUR

Dario's gunshots had drawn the cops; a higher force led them. The first wave wasn't cops, exactly; instead a group of Bajan commandos arrived and formed a defensive perimeter, their leader quickly identifying Dahl and treating him as one of their own. All a result of Jo's forewarning, Dahl's incoming team had alerted the Bajan commandos and enlisted their help.

"Who sent you?"

"Came down the wires. Over the waves." The commando smiled. "Someone has been watching Prime Minister Sealy for a long time now, hoping to catch the men who owned him. Turns out," a slight pause. "All they needed to do was call you."

Dahl still didn't trust the new man entirely, but he knew Jo had called the team and, indirectly, hopefully this was the back-up. "Give me a name."

The commando spoke one five-letter surname and all was well, since it was a name Dahl trusted with his life. Dahl relaxed and pointed to the dead body. "That one's Gabrio Vega, cartel boss. He still has a few men running around the island somewhere, probably looking for the coast." He smiled to convey the joke.

Dario said, "I killed him."

Dahl grimaced. "We'll get to that. The other man there is Nick Grant. He's a fixer, of sorts. One of the worst gutter-crawlers alive. I do believe he's one of the Top Ten."

"You're referring to the FBI's Most Wanted list?"

"No, the other one. Signed off by the President."

The commando looked impressed. "Wow."

"Easy for you to say."

"That alone guarantees your safety," the commando said. "If we recognized your President's authority. Which we don't."

"You work for Sealy then?"

A nod. "We do."

Dahl re-evaluated the distance to weapons, the caliber of this man, the positioning of his team, the best route of escape. Against that, he weighed Jo's call to the team and the team's decision to send the commandos.

"But we can't find Sealy," the man went on. "So the situation's under my control. For now."

Dahl nodded. "My guess? The bastard's long gone. You can find my ID back in the hotel room's safe."

"Agent?"

"Special Forces," He held out a hand. "Torsten Dahl."

"And your family?" The commando shot a glance over at the exact place where Dahl had secreted them.

"Just that. My family. This is our vacation."

A laugh. "Some trip. You like it extreme?"

"Always."

"What do you guys do for Christmas?"

"We blow shit up."

"Cool. Cool. Us too. So, are you ready to tell me what the hell happened?"

Dahl noticed that Grant was starting to stir. "I am, but first will you cuff that asshat for me? Really tight. To a tree or something. You can't let him slip away."

The commando signaled to his men, who ran over to Grant, gear jangling as they moved.

Dahl eyed the commando. Could he trust this man? Everything he'd done today had been to save his family, even the comeback of the soldier and the Mad Swede. The unbreakable root that firmed up and guided everything he did was his children.

"Seriously," he said. "I've found only one man I can

trust on this island today," he nodded at Dario. "And he's the son of a Mexican cartel chief."

The commando actually laughed. "Now there's some irony, man. But hell, what else do I have to do?"

Dahl understood. A trustworthy name had been mentioned. No weapons leveled. No cuffs presented. They knew where his family were hidden yet hadn't made a move. Grant had been secured, as requested.

Options clicked through his head like rolling symbols in a slot machine.

"We could talk," he said. "You and I. Over there."

Closer to the sea, away from potential turncoats and any form of back-up. The commandos' leader would be putting his own life on the line, alone with Dahl. The risks were high, but trust had never been more important.

The commando stripped off all his communication devices but kept hold of his weapons. "I hear your friends are inbound. The team you called. Is this really necessary?"

They walked in silence for a while, ever closer to the lapping waves. A fresh, cool air embraced them, promising relaxation, safety and a change from the norm.

"D'you know?" Dahl said. "This is the first vacation I've had in years."

"I can see why."

"Nothing has ended well," Dahl said ruefully. "Not really. My family are safe and that's the blessing, but some enemies remain and others are still free. This is how real life goes. It's not all beautifully wrapped in the end. There will always be threats to soldiers like you and I, and different people have different anxieties. It's all relative."

"We do it for those who can't," the Bajan commando said. "To keep our way of life safe. To keep the crazies away."

Right then, Dahl knew he could trust the man. "What's your name, pal?"

"Ambrose," he said. "Kai Ambrose."

"Well, well, Mr. Ambrose. Do I have a story for you . . ."

FORTY FIVE

Much later, Dahl thought back over the day and wondered when he'd accepted that he was entirely human. Working constantly with an expert team of warriors, problem-solvers and decision-makers tended to warp a man's sense of himself, Dahl now understood. The truth was, something existed that could always bring him straight down to earth and set his foundations crumbling.

Well, two somethings.

The hotel room felt like an alien environment, cool, locked, safe, normal. They'd been allowed to return after an exhaustive conversation. There were armed guards outside the door and around the hotel, either to keep the Dahls in or to protect them. It was hard to say. His special team had now arrived and were also in discussions, but Dahl and Johanna and Dario had said all they could.

For today.

The night was almost beyond its expiration date, clinging on grimly like a man afraid to let go of an old image of himself. It dripped silently down the horizon, stealing away. Dahl and Johanna sat on the edge of their bed, the children close and dozing under the covers, the family not wanting to be parted now for even half a second.

"About the marriage thing," Johanna said simply, staring into space. "I believe I said I wanted to be alone. That we should take a break. I think now that maybe I was wrong."

Dahl knew they'd all changed—but he was still learning in exactly what ways. "I was wrong too. About so many things, Jo. You can't always be a soldier. You can't always be a father, the man they want to see. You have to switch between both like a bloody magician."

"Sooner or later, they will need to see the real world." she thought about the day they'd had and added: "A *different* real world."

"Yeah, true, but not yet, eh? Their innocence is their spirit, it keeps it all so precious."

"Hell, you're such a softie. If only the bad guys could see you now."

"Let's not wish for any more of that. It seems that you can look after me as well as I can look after you. Now, there's a future together we never knew."

She laughed and shaded her eyes theatrically. "I can see it!"

"It's odd. We can see it now but not 24 hours ago."

"Perspectives have changed."

"We're standing our ground."

"Are we?"

"As a unit. A marriage. A family. We're holding on, breaking through. We're making our stand. Yesterday, against criminals. Tomorrow, between ourselves. It's—"

"All relative," Johanna smiled. "Yes, I know."

"Other things may come and go." Dahl saw the first bloom of a new sunrise startle the horizon. "They may mingle. Situations may arise. Absences. Worry. But we'll stand strong and make it through."

Johanna laid her head on his arm. "I believe that we will."

Dahl then felt one of the most simple and yet best and warmest sensations that life had ever offered — the loving feel of his child's arms wrapping around his shoulders.

"I love you, Daddy," Isabella murmured, still mostly asleep.

All his worries fell away as the new day began to dawn.

THE END

David Leadbeater

David Leadbeater is the author of nineteen Kindle International Bestsellers since 2012. To view them please see the list below. To view a chronological reading order please visit his website:
www.davidleadbeater.com

Beyond that look out for the latest news and regular, signed paperback giveaways on his Facebook page:
https://www.facebook.com/davidleadbeaternovels/

As always, genuine e-mails are welcomed and replied to within a few days. If you have any questions please drop him a line: davidleadbeater2011@homail.co.uk

And please remember:
Reviews are everything to an author and essential to the future of the Torsten Dahl, Matt Drake, Alicia Myles and other series. Please consider leaving even a few lines at Amazon, it will make all the difference.

Other Books by David Leadbeater:

The Matt Drake Series
The Bones of Odin (Matt Drake #1)
The Blood King Conspiracy (Matt Drake #2)
The Gates of hell (Matt Drake 3)
The Tomb of the Gods (Matt Drake #4)
Brothers in Arms (Matt Drake #5)
The Swords of Babylon (Matt Drake #6)
Blood Vengeance (Matt Drake #7)
Last Man Standing (Matt Drake #8)
The Plagues of Pandora (Matt Drake #9)
The Lost Kingdom (Matt Drake #10)
The Ghost Ships of Arizona (Matt Drake #11)
The Last Bazaar (Matt Drake #12)
Edge of Armageddon (Matt Drake #13)

The Alicia Myles Series
Aztec Gold (Alicia Myles #1)
Crusader's Gold (Alicia Myles #2)

The Disavowed Series:
The Razor's Edge (Disavowed #1)
In Harm's Way (Disavowed #2)
Threat Level: Red (Disavowed #3)

David Leadbeater

The Chosen Few Series
Chosen (The Chosen Trilogy #1)
Guardians (The Chosen Tribology #2)

Short Stories
Walking with Ghosts (A short story)
A Whispering of Ghosts (A short story)

Connect with the author on Twitter: @dleadbeater2011
Visit the author's website: **www.davidleadbeater.com**

All helpful, genuine comments are welcome. I would love
to hear from you.
davidleadbeater2011@hotmail.co.uk

Made in the USA
Middletown, DE
27 December 2023